Praise for *...Let Us Not Be Afraid*

"Abeyta's prose is beautifully rendered, each new chapter standing alone as a long poem...[the novel has a] Faulkner-inspired sense of the wholeness of a village voice."

Rocky Mountain News

"Abeyta has written a novel that reads like narrative poetry, epic in subject, biblical in implication."

Annie Dawid, *High Country News*

"This mix of history and fiction and myth reminds me so much of Gabriel Garcia Marquez and his magical realism... it's worth the effort as you see a community develop into a character, and share the frequent sorrows and occasional joys of life in some hard country."

Ed Quillen, *Colorado Central Magazine*

"[Abeyta is a] very talented writer...his voice is unique and adventurous: very much Southern Colorado (El Valle de San Luis, actually), and very much in touch with the passions of the Valley gente.

Manuel Ramos, *La Bloga*

"Striking."—*Aspen Times*

Rise,

Do Not Be

Afraid

A Novel

aaron a. abeyta

GHOST ROAD PRESS

Library of Congress Cataloging-in-Publication Data.
aaron a. abeyta
   Rise, Do Not Be Afraid.

Ghost Road Press
ISBN 0978945689 (Trade Paperback)
Library of Congress Control Number: 2006938574

Book Design: Sonya Unrein
Cover photo: David Guerrero

Ghost Road Press, Denver, Colorado
ghostroadpress.com

Also by Aaron A. Abeyta

colcha
as orion falls

For Always Michele

Contents

Dramatis Personae

Nonnatusia—Loves Ramon.

Ramon Fernandez—Loves Nonnatusia; Nephew to Nomio.

Nomio –A great sheepherder; Ramon's Uncle.

Apollonio—Oldest of the village elders.

Mana Virginia—Village elder and curandera.

Aresando—War veteran in love with Malinche-Santistevan Matthews.

Malinche Santistevan-Matthews—Believes she is the descendant of Spanish royalty.

Samuel & Elle—Gossips who get their news by listening to crickets; parents of Aresando.

Ambrose Benedict-Matthews—Greedy land speculator from Chicago.

Ponce Santistevan-Matthews—Malinche's father.

Karl Varshant—Malinche's husband.

Thomas B. Catlin—Obtained all the land in and around Santa Rita.

Rafael Trujillo—The great pianist who plays with Nomio and Apollonio.

Carillo—The greatest of the sheepherders; taught Nomio how to herd.

Esperanza—A classmate of Nonnatusia's.

Enos—Nomio's Grandfather who takes in the bueyeros.

Edimundo—The pitcher for the Santa Rita baseball team.

Pelayo—Nomio's father.

Adelaida—Nomio's mother.

Cassiano—World's worst fisherman.

Rosa—Cassiano's wife.

Blaesilla—A widow with many sons

Jose Francisco –Baseball player that negotiates with the bueyeros.

Juan Sanchez—The best farmer in Santa Rita.

Dionicio—Owner of El Rio Lounge, a womanizer.

Known Only to God

Of the three, two are named, and one is known only to God. Two, the named, are buried together beneath a cedar tree on land his abuelito bought from a woman named Lara. Like two of the three that he never imagined or knew, he also did not know Lara, but he used to play in her hollowed-out house, drop dark round stones into her unused well and wait for the sound of the stone's heart to beat as it entered the water.

Lara's house was built south of the mesa that looms over his boyhood home. During the winter there are parts of the earth beneath that mesa that never feel the sun. Lara's house is just beyond the winter reach of the mesa's shadow. The cedar tree where the two are buried is not. All of the earth below the mesa is covered with and full of stones, cold round river stones smoothed gray with shades of black and red, left there by an ancient river. The river still exists, further down from the mesa it flows less violently, thinner, greener, less than a quarter mile from where it left its memory, its round and water pocked children of stone. Despite the rocks, people were always digging. Men mostly, with their shovels, talaches, and fierros, have put up homes, dug wells, buried children, left rounded ditches as proof of their work.

The cedar tree sits between two ditches, one large and stony as its old mother, the other shallow and clay formed. During the winter the tree does not feel the sun. He dug one grave, a January grave in the frozen earth between those two acequias. For all his life in that cañon, it will be the only lasting proof of his ever living or working there, that shallow cedar-shaded grave between two ditches where two of the three are buried and are with him now helping tell this story. Whatever voice you hear, it may be theirs, the abandoned well's, the mostly forgotten adobe home's, the winter shadow's, the ancient river's or the voices of two acequias; whatever voice you hear, you must know that it is also God's.

He chose that tree because it is near his mother and father's house. It is near the field where he once played. He thought the memory of young voices playing off the walls of the mesa would be like bells from a far away church, the kind you hear randomly and distantly but recognize nonetheless, so too are the voices and joyful screams of youth against cliffs of hardened clay and always green arms of cedar.

The third was not dreamt or named. The third received no blessing from the priest, only those of its mother and father, tears. Again, a January burial almost exactly one year removed from the two. He built a fire with wood from his woodpile, pino, piñon, aspen, cottonwood, and cedar. He built the fire on the llano on a hill where the earth took its time. He built the fire in a place where there is far sight to the east and shelter from the winds always blowing from the west. Here the earth rises slowly, almost imperceptibly, until it reaches two small cerritos, again a place he once loved in youth. At the base of the southern cerrito he built that fire of five woods, starting slowly like his abuelita used to do, with palitos of aspen, soft as reeds, and then adding pino chopped thin and full of ocote, until the flames popped and the fire began to glow from its center, its heart of embers where the soft stringy cottonwood would rest and begin to burn like shriveling paper. Of all the wood the cottonwood burns the poorest, but it is the wood of the riverbank, the wood that is in abundance, the only wood truly from home. Therefore, the cottonwood is necessary and almost sacred. He built the fire of five woods on an imperceptible hill where the earth took its time, finally adding the piñon, which burns hot as coal. Then he added the cedar, which scented the llano air with its smoke.

His abuelita saved buttons, empty coffee cans, band-aid tins, jelly jars washed clean, rags from torn shirts, she saved and saved because in her world there was nothing like poverty, rather it was a wealth of necessity. There were always too many needs to be met and sometimes there were only mismatched buttons to fill the gaps of her and her children's existence. Nothing was ever thrown away after only one use. There was always a reason to save what no one else wanted.

Sometimes that part of her found its way into him, the part that took the cold ashes of the third and delicately scooped them into an empty coffee can, washed clean by the sweet well water of his abuelita's empty house. He brought the ashes to their mother. She placed the can safely in her closet.

The dark circle where the fire burned is buried beneath a mound of fine, yet heavy, llano soil. On the mound he placed thirteen stones in the shape of a cross, knowing that nothing would disturb them.

Sometime during the summer that came to the valley

of Santa Rita, he took the ashes of the third to the highest place he knew, the place where water is born, the place where the river and the acequias begin. He trusted the third to the water. What begins up there, in high western mountains named for a saint, will flow north into the river of stones and then move east as it drops toward the valleys and meadows of his home. From the meadows, human hands will divert the river's blood into hundreds of acequias, two of them passing the place where the other two are buried; finally the water will meet itself again and continue east toward an even older river that flows south and cuts a gorge of black volcanic rock in two. West of that dark rocked gorge the earth slowly rises toward the place where the dark circle of the third's fire looks east and thus completes everything without ever entering the sky.

The hardest question for him to answer was also the most common: "Do you have any kids?"

There was no easy way to answer. No matter how much he ignored them, everyone around him would not cease. They talked of everyone else's children unaware that words, like questions, hurt. There was no easy way to answer the simplest question. Yes required many words. No was a lie. He chose yes because he had not done the work that remains even after the builder has left. He chose yes because there were stories in the highest places, in the water, in the places where the earth begins slowly to rise. There were many names known only to God.

How the Word Should Rise

The word should come like water rising, something slight as the thin notes of a violin played by a little girl standing on a stump, her soft grainy song floating over an open field of grass. The word should come like snow falling for the first time. It was October, 1958, when the snow began during that first week. From up high the herders began to move their borregas toward the lights of town. Ramon Fernandez did not come down that year. Some said that they should go for his body with the first melt of spring. Nomio, with the huge hat and beautiful boots, told the others that he would gather the body the next day. Too much snow, they said. Too many words uttered about two bodies rather than one. He assured them that he would deliver Ramon Fernandez to his home.

Nomio received his enormous hat and shiny boots from God. They were always clean, the envy of every man in Santa Rita.

Here, the roads, in the right light of morning, just after the earth has exhaled its warm breath into the cold morning air, just as the sun hits the dirt and gravel, the roads begin to sparkle as if from diamonds. It was these very roads that convinced Nomio to gather the body of Ramon Fernandez.

"Ramon Fernandez is nobody," they told him.

Nomio would later attribute his actions to the limping fences or the abandoned buildings of home, but in the deep well of his being it was the roads lined with broken bottles that put him on his palomina mare.

Venus burned in the clear morning. Nomio's breath mingled with the breath of his best horse. They rode west away from Venus, and like the fog of their breathing, the two were one and moving quickly. In the valley there was no snow; Nomio reined the palomina in. He said nothing, but patted her neck, his palm telling her that the day would be long. She was his best horse and therefore knew him better than any human. She slowed to a fast walk as Venus burned itself into the horizon of the San Juans. The day would be clear. The snow would be wet. They turned southwest toward los brazos.

Ramon Fernandez had not always been nobody. The women of Santa Rita remembered that he could dance well. He carried a wooden rosary in one pocket, a small knife in the other. Ramon Fernandez, before he was nobody, was like the people of Santa Rita, rich with no money. The tragedy began long before the diamond roads caught the sun.

Before there were roads and fences, you could look west from a field that belonged to Ramon's father. A person could look west along the path of the rio where horses worked their tails in the pre summer heat, the mosquitoes laddered themselves in the warm air and the lirios bent soft purple toward the clover and brome. The water from the river rose in the acequias slowly, cold as its winter mother.

"La acequia esta viva."

Ramon would shout it toward home and his daughter

would jump on the stump of an old cottonwood outside their adobe. Her Christmas gift was only slightly too big for her, but she loved its four strings, its hollow body, its thin voice, her own small distorted reflection in the lacquer, and so she would play for the water rising into the meadows, for her father standing in the cold water. She played and played the only song she knew. It was something sad, her father's song.

It was the girl that Nomio remembered as la palomina entered the bare and ivory aspens. He wondered if word had reached her. Nomio wondered about her violin and what songs, if any, she still played.

The Lamp of Your Body

Luke 11:34

People always say that the people of Santa Rita are different. They say it in a way that is good. They speak of themselves as though the mountains do not let anything but the snow and wind in.

There are five ingredients for tortillas. Too often the people think of themselves as only one ingredient. The truth is that the people of Santa Rita do not like to be called Mexican.

"We don't speak Mexican Spanish."

"We don't even speak Spanish Spanish."

"There is no one in the world like us."

Of all the words, only those last ones are probably true.

Start with flour, the kind our abuelita scoops out with a tin cup, always the same cup, always the same tin cup balanced in her hand, not really measured but weighed by the soft thin fingers of her hands holding the tin cup, balanced really between the farmer's grain, the earth's rain, the acequias rising, the counter clockwise walking of the horses in the mill, balanced there between what has been mentioned and what has been forgotten.

Then take those same hands, feel the papery skin, feel the ridges of her nails, feel the veins rising on her hand. Take those same hands and knead in the manteca, the same manteca the little boy strained into the empty coffee can our abuelita saved, the same manteca from the marano whose hair is scalded off with boiling water, whose skin is cut into squares on a Saturday afternoon, invite all your vecinos, build a fire beneath a great black caldera, let the pig hang in the soterrano, but bring the squares of cuero and drop them in the caldera, play some music, put pico de gallo in a clay bowl, send the youngest into the house for some cut lime and some salt, everyone talk as the chicharrones crackle, give your vecina con las tortillas de maiz the spot closest to the fire, place the chicharrones in the tortilla, a little pico too, some lime, and then the salt, then down. Let everything cool and then send the youngest boy to strain the manteca into old coffee cans and empty jars. Later, our abuelita will knead it into the harina poured from the tin cup.

Add the salt, the same salt our abuelita sent the youngest for that Saturday. This too she will measure by the balance of it in a cupped hand. She'll think of Jesus. "I love you like bread loves salt." She'll think of the oceans, the dark boats with white sails that her father's name came over on, she'll think of waves coming ashore, she'll think of her ancient mother's home and the things they would trade for salt, she'll think royalty, she'll think of Neruda's ode, she'll think of how she measures her own life in her hand, she'll think that of all the beauty in the world, salt is the one Jesus chose for love.

The next ingredient is often the most forgotten, like the Indio in us; it is small but no less important than the others. Our abuelita will cup it between two of her fingers, again a balance, the bequenpaura there above the bowl is the difference between crackers and perfection. Don't forget the espauda because it colors your blood and makes you love the earth, sometimes it makes you quiet but mostly it makes you rise perfectly.

Then there is the lamp of our body, our abuelita's eyes and all the water they have seen, the softness of them like the lakes of los brazos, or the darkness of them in a spring river passing, but mostly her eyes are warm and many colored rings of an old and beautiful tree that records the water for each year of its growing. The water must be warm like when all of us were born. The warm water must be mixed in slowly like the patience of snow melting in May and finally warming in July. The water is what makes this place different, the water is the only ingredient we add in doses, not too much, slow and warm, the water must be added slow and warm, the water is the part the men understand, the water is what our abuelita will save for last, the body is mostly water, the body's lamp is water that pools in the eyes, it is proof of pain, happiness, love, loss, it is warm and must be kneaded into the rest of our lives. Without water there would be no trinity of left hand right hand comal. Watch as our abuelita, the part of our being that respects the earth, slowly adds water to her mixture, watch as the water makes the table and bolio necessary, watch as the tortilla spreads itself over the wooden table like water running into a field.

The lamp of our body is the eyes. Watch the water. It makes us possible. It makes this place and people rise together and not be afraid.

The Cost of Five Sparrows

Luke 12:7

The crickets were singing wildly in the adobe walls. Samuel and Elle sat at their wooden table smashing piñon with a shared bolio. Both of them were old, neither wishing to risk their precious teeth on the dark brown seeds.

"You hear what they're saying," he asked?

"That they will be leaving soon, now that it is getting cold."

"Yes that, but the other thing."

"How do you think they know that?" Elle popped four piñon into her mouth, the smashed shells, sucked of their salt, rising in a small mound to her left.

"The moon I suppose. That is how I would know if I were them."

"You think he will be okay?"

"What's all the damn banging in here?" It was Aresando, Samuel and Elle's son.

"Sorry, mijo. We are nervous. You know how your mom and I get when they sing so loud. We had to do something. Piñon?" He offered it in his round hand as though it were spare change. He offered it the way a father offers things to a son before the son has grown and left. Maybe now that

Aresando was back from the war the two of them could fish together again.

Aresando did not acknowledge the offer. He was looking far beyond his father, far beyond the cricket-filled walls.

"He is traveling," Elle whispered.

Samuel brought the piñon back into his closed hand. He held it there like the small round seeds of a wish.

"Do I, pues what should I do?"

"Let him go. He'll be back soon." She placed a piñon in front of her and with one whack the bolio split the shell. The piñon was roasted perfectly. She brought the cracked seed to her mouth, tasted the salt and lingered on it, her lips pursing, her tongue working its way into the cracked seed like melt water into a frozen stone.

"Como agua," she said. "He will be back." She pounded another seed.

"Como agua," he repeated.

"People think I'm crazy, but I don't believe that crickets speak to me. I don't even believe I can talk about someone while they are standing right in front of me. I don't think I can talk about someone who is standing right in front of me and not think they heard me. Now that is crazy. Me, I'm just out of place." Aresando walked to the only door in the house. When he opened it the moon reflected in the glass above the doorknob. He walked into the late summer night, past where the moon would allow his mother to follow with her eyes.

"Close the door, Viejo. They will tell us where he went."

"There is too much out there. How could they keep track?"

"The moon. Just like you said."

Aresando was out of place, but he was crazy too. He walked into the night. It was 1953 and the dreams of the hands were still with him. It was the dreams that made him crazy. It was the dreams that made him walk toward the notes of Apollonio's crooked guitar, the sound floating through the cantina door and into the night.

He hadn't been born crazy. He was born on Palm Sunday, 1932. Samuel left the house late on the Saturday, which preceded the celebration of Jesus riding a donkey into Jerusalem. Samuel walked down to the corral he had built with his father when he was ten. That was a good year, but he didn't think of that. He saddled their only animal, a dark mule he had named Baby. He whispered to the mule as he saddled her. He apologized for coming so late in the night, for bringing her out in the cold. It was going to snow. The air was flat and almost warm. It was the dead air before a big snow. He explained to Baby that Elle needed Mana Virginia, that their boy was being born.

Samuel walked the three miles quickly. Inside Virginia's house the light of a kerosene lamp was already jumping and reflecting into the night. She met him at the door, ready before he even asked.

El Sanador was named Raphael Parra. He was a great healer with an even greater horse, a great black horse, taller than most men. The horse had long legs that moved beautifully, strong. The horse never grew tired of bringing the old man to the villages. Raphael Parra lived in Tres Piedras, a thirty-mile ride to Santa Rita. Raphael means God Heals. Likely, Raphael Parra's mother had named him appropriately back in 1860, the twenty-ninth of September. San Rafael, the patron saint of the blind and of travelers, had blessed Raphael Parra with a different kind of sight, a second sight. He had also blessed him with the most beautiful horse anyone had ever seen, so the old doctor could travel well. It was 1902 when Raphael Parra used his second sight to pick Virginia. This sight of his had told him that he only had ten years left. He even knew the day, the 19th of December. It also told him that his great black horse, Oeste, would die within the year.

San Rafael always traveled with a staff, a stick really, which he showed to Raphael in a dream. It would be raining, twins being born in San Miguel. In the dream he cut through the trees, because it was raining and because it was quicker. San Rafael showed him the stick in the dream, placed it in the tall grass next to some aspen. He placed the stick on top of the hill, right before the descent into San Miguel. Raphael saw it in his dream, the same way he dreamt the twins being born.

Raphael rose from his wool filled camalta. He knew as he saddled the black that this was the last time. The horse knew too. Neither protested the rain or the will of the patron saint. Oeste glided over the wet rocks and chamizo. It was a twenty-three mile ride to San Miguel, only twenty to the top of the hill. Raphael saw the spot, recognized the aspen trees clearly; one had Dios Es Amor carved into the white bark, the other tree proclaimed that *RF* loved *NT*. It would have been easy enough to veer away, but the saint's stick would move with them, even the people without the dream sight knew this. Oeste was moving fast. He was beautiful in the rain. With his left hoof the great black horse came down on the end of the saint's staff and it shot up as Oeste glided into it, the opposite end of the staff found the animal's belly, the weight of the great horse driving the stick cleanly into the body where it broke in two. As Oeste fell, the broken end, with the impact of the wet earth and the horse's body, razored upward into the heart of the most beautiful horse anyone had ever seen.

Raphael had seen the horse's death and his own long before he ever met Virginia. He had seen her too, also in a dream. He knew that Virginia had the same sight as he had. He pretended to teach her so the people of Santa Rita would come to her without hesitation, but the earth was already in Virginia. She knew innately, like the earth's spinning, what healed.

Virginia placed the zalea beneath Elle, the tanned side up. Samuel waited in the only other room of the house, the kitchen. Something told him to boil water. He filled every olla in the house and put them on the wood stove. The kitchen seemed made of steam. Virginia worked in the other room at the pace of the earth. The boy would emerge only when everything was ready.

"He will come right before the sun." Virginia's announcement almost made Elle smile.

There were no clocks in the house, but everything in the world was silent. Outside, only the approaching snow moved, and Aresando was born that morning of Palm Sunday right before the sun rose above the Sangre de Cristos and right as the snow began to fall.

"He's not crying. He's not crying. Dime, what's wrong?"

"He is breathing fine. He is healthy, but you should know this one will not cry."

Virginia tied the boy's umbligo into a knot and called for Samuel. He came into the room shriveled and soaked from the steam, but he smiled and ran out of the room. He returned with three bags in his left hand. One by one he transferred them to his right and handed them to Virginia. The first was a bag of piñon, the second filled with beans.

"The piñon is already done, Mana Virginia, and I already cleaned the beans, no rocks, no bad ones. They are ready to eat, both of them are ready to eat. Well not the beans, those need cooking, but they're clean. Tu Sabes, ready."

The third bag was the smallest. It made the noise of coins

that had been saved for nine months.

"It is all we have for now, but I can get more."

"No te figas Samuel, con los frijoles voy contenta."

"He's not crying." Samuel had finally noticed.

"This one will not cry Samuel, but he is fine."

"Never cry? Pues my boy will be a real man."

"No. A real man will look after his wife after a long night. This one is just a baby. He will learn from you how to be a man. He just won't cry."

Virginia was right. There was nothing wrong with Aresando. His eyes pooled when the wind blew or when sleep was coming, but he never once cried.

In time, Aresando fell in love. Her name was Malinche Santistevan-Matthews. She had green eyes. Everyone in Santa Rita had brown eyes, but hers were green and she knew that made her destined to be lucky. She told everyone that she was a descendant of royalty. The king of Spain had sent them here because the king loved them. Malinche Santistevan-Matthews only repeated what her father told her.

Ponce Santistevan-Matthews had sold everything early on. The land was not for royalty to work, so he sold everything to his father in-law, Ambrose Benedict Matthews whose family had arrived from Chicago in 1878, when Ambrose was five. Ambrose Benedict Matthews agreed with Ponce Santistevan-Matthews, royalty or the descendants of royalty should not have to work. Ambrose Benedict-Matthews bought a thousand acres from Ponce for $917. To sweeten the pot, Ambrose Benedict-Matthews also promised Ponce Santistevan the hand of his daughter, his only child, making sure that as part of the deal Ponce Santistevan would take the Matthews name too, because it is Mexican tradition he said, and for posterity. For posterity, Ambrose Benedict Matthews wasted no time fencing his new land.

That was 1926, and because Ponce Santistevan would no longer need it, he took Ponce's water, also for posterity.

So Aresando loved the green eyed future queen of Spain and would do anything to impress her. He didn't care that every boy in school loved her too. He didn't care that Ponce's house was made of wood and nails, that it had five rooms and you didn't have to eat in the kitchen. He didn't care that Malinche Santistevan-Matthews was already planning to leave Santa Rita for a city that suited her place in the order of things. Aresando Vargas would not cry for Malinche Santistevan-Matthews, but he was brave enough to do anything else.

Bravery. That's what Ulises Urea noticed first in Aresando Vargas.

Santa Rita sat in a long and deep canyon cut by an ancient river of ice, now melted to a river that flowed east toward the Rio Grande. The canyon was deep, flanked by two tall mesas. There was no TV reception in Santa Rita. Most news traveled like it always had, by word of mouth, from one man to the next, usually originating with Samuel who had heard it from the crickets. It was the crickets that told Samuel that Aresando was going to join the Marines, to impress a girl.

"Your son is brave sir. I watched him on the football field. Nothing slows him down. Helluva blitzer, excuse my language sir, but that is what we need, brave blitzers."

"Blitz ni Blitz. I've heard from…" Samuel paused here to let himself acknowledge his company and determine that this recruiter would not understand the crickets as a reputable source. "I've heard in the papers about your war."

"Sir, with all due respect, your son is quite intelligent. Someone with his brains would most likely work with electronics. He'd be totally safe."

"Now he is smart. You said brave before. Don't think I don't know how the government works. Look around you

Sergeant Urea. You know why the roads glitter in the sun? I'll tell you. They glitter because that is how you trick us, with glitter. Mira que shiny you say. Look, todo esto, all this glittered away from us, y pa que, a little feria, a little gold. Now you want my son. You glitter him with gold you wear on your sleeves."

"Sir, he will be defending our country, representing the United States of America, representing Santa Rita. He'll make you proud."

"I've been proud since 1932. No gold bars made of lana gonna make me more proud."

"Sir, your son has already signed. He wants to go."

Samuel turned to Aresando. His face was blank, but his eyes spoke first. Signed?

"You signed?"

"Si papá."

"How many times I told you. Never sign anything. Ink don't get you nothing, mijo. I know. Mira." He pointed toward Santa Rita. "Ink will dry and anything dry is poor."

"I want to go, papá."

"For a girl who thinks she is a princess?"

"That's not why."

"See, you sign something and already you are lying to your familia."

"I already signed."

"We can kill him, throw him in the river, burn that paper."

Ulises Urea had stood up in case he had to defend himself. He was an average sized man, gone from his family for ten years. He no longer knew how to interpret a father's plea. He only heard threats and only knew to respond with fire.

Apollonio was playing his crooked guitar when Aresando walked into the cantina. There wasn't a lot of smoke so everything seemed clear in the kerosene light of five faroles.

Dionicio was behind the bar. Aresando ordered two whiskeys and a glass of water. Rafael Trujillo had come in behind Aresando and took his seat at the piano. No one knew who played better, Apollonio or Rafael. Together they played beautifully, old songs that no one knew the words to, songs that were like history or a newspaper you happen upon many years later, one you saved for some reason you can't remember but recognize and still read for its truth. Both men began to play, but Aresando hardly listened. In truth he preferred Nomio's guitara de los dos cuernos. Nomio's guitara de los dos cuernos was in the corner as Apollonio and Rafael played something slow and full of pain.

Aresando finished his second whiskey and ordered another. He felt nothing, completely normal, as he walked over to Apollonio who had just finished playing his crooked guitar. Apollonio had been in many wars. He was the best shot in Santa Rita.

"Do you think I'm crazy?"

"Not always, but you are now."

"Do you think that God watches over us?"

"You are still alive. That must mean something."

"But I'm not right anymore."

"You weren't meant to stay right. You are something else now."

"You know those five mud nests outside under the techo. You think God watches those five birds and their babies?"

"They are still alive."

"If I went out there right now and broke those nests would God still be watching over them?"

"I suppose if killing those five sparrows made you feel better, then I believe he would be watching over you."

Mark Well How the Lilies Grow

Luke 12:27

~~Dear Nonnatusia,~~
~~Hello, how are you?~~
~~Dear Nonnatusia,~~
~~This is Ramon Fernandez, you know~~
~~Dear Nonnatusia,~~
~~I have been wanting to write you for awhile~~

Dear Nonnatusia,

Do you remember in the 5th grade when Mrs. Trujillo read to us from that German poet's book? She said he died in 1926. I remember because that was the year I was born. You too, we were in the same grade, except your birthday is August 31st. I remember because they announced it in church. I write stuff like that down.

Anyway, Mrs. Trujillo told us he died of something in his blood. Do you remember that poem about the lion in a cage? That's not really what I'm writing about, but I remember when the German poet was dying he got a letter from a woman. The letter said that the German was not her favorite poet. That doesn't seem nice, you know, because he was dying and it hurt, but she said something like this. You are not my favorite poet. You are poetry.

I hope you are still reading this. I remember all that stuff because it was the first day I really noticed you, February 23rd. I remember thinking that the German was poetry and he had something in his blood. I remember because there was something in my blood that day, like when the river gets full and cold, like that. Anyway, Mrs. Trujillo told us a lot that day, but I only remember the German because I felt like that lion in the poem, the one in the cage, and since then you have been love to me the way that German was poetry to the lady who sent the letter. So I guess I know I have felt this way for almost six years now, and you know that a full river, if it is full too long, it washes away the land. So what do you think? ~~Do you~~ Maybe I can come by and see you sometime.

~~Love Your Fr~~

With ~~Affection~~ Admiration

Ramon

Dip the Tip of Your Finger
in Water and Cool My Tongue

Luke 16:24

It was one of those stars that pulses like a heart going out, slow and red. Enos watched the stars. He didn't know their names, but he knew their turning, their passage through the night. He had one son, a boy, Pelayo, four years old, born in 1874 during a November like this one. The star was in the south, above San Antonio Mountain. It pulsed like a slow heart; he knew they would be tired.

The bueyeros all looked hungry when they arrived. There were thirteen families. Seventy-four people in all. Enos had seen others, but none this hungry, none this late in the year.

The star in the south had throbbed all summer. The lirios and the grass in his meadow had grown thick this year. Apollonio had told him that they would be coming and what they would want. Enos had twenty-two cows. Apollonio had fifty, but he would not share them. He believed that they prayed to another god. The red star was almost gone for the winter when the bueyeros arrived. For a week before they arrived, Enos kept his knife sharp.

In one hand he carried a bucket and in his right a single shot rifle his father had given him. The base of the cottonwood was stained black and the branch that they used had a groove burned into it by the rope.

There was no green in the meadow, but the steer ran into the field anyway, grazing on the brown grass. Enos had attached his tiro de caballos to the wagon and guided them next to the steer. From the seat he again took up the bucket and the single shot. He carried them in the same hands as before. When the animal looked up, it finally noticed it was alone, turning its head toward the twenty-one still locked in the corral. Beyond the corral, to the east, three of the women from the wagons and Enos' wife, Cirila, were making a fire. Pelayo and two of the wagon boys were trying to catch smoke in their small hands. Enos checked the wagon's brake with his eyes. Two of the bueyeros had come to hold the horses. On the west side of the field there were four others, waiting at the tree. From the direction of the smoke, two others walked slowly toward the steer. From the corral the steer's mother was bramando and the dark red novillo with the white face answered his mother. Enos whistled, the rifle already at his shoulder. The novillo turned toward him and then fell before the echo of the bala came back. Enos placed the bucket at the steer's neck and cut to the jugular with the knife he had kept sharp for a week. The novillo's heart was still beating; the blood gushed into the bucket. The novillo's legs began to move. He was running. The bullet had gone directly into the brain. It was his heart telling him to run, but he only thrashed there in the gold grass. Each of the Bueyeros took a leg and held it, cutting crosswise the tendon where the leg met the hoof. The novillo quit running and its open neck sucked at the air. Enos rose from his bucket of blood and went to each leg. With his own knife he cut vertically. He smiled at one of the men.

"Four crosses." He consciously spoke in English.

The man smiled back and then all five of them pulled the limp novillo onto the wagon. They took the novillo to the stained tree. From the wagon, Enos and the man who smiled lifted the steer while the seven on the ground pulled the rope tied to the steer's hind leg. They tied the rope off and two of the bueyeros took the wagon back to the corral and unhitched the horses. One of them unlatched the gate and the steer's mother ran to the blood spattered grass. The other cows followed her until they got the scent. All of them ran, bucking and bramando to the far end of the field. All the cows would be wild until the scent left them. By spring all of the cows would stain the tree. Only humans walk toward the scent of death. As they bucked by, the novillo hung from the tree. Its steaming organs and stomach were piled on the blood wet-hide, laid flat beneath the steer's dead eyes.

The bueyeros from Mississippi thanked Enos profusely as they ate around the fire. They promised to repay him and he accepted their offer, sure that one day his family might be lost too, or hungry or thirsty.

Apollonio sang alone in the cantina that night. He sang his corrido about the steer that was sacrificed. Apollonio did not even bother to change the names. The news traveled from the cantina that night. His song went like this:

> Era el dia veintiuno de Noviembre
> Cuando llegaron los muertos de hambre
> En su vegita, el Enos los dio lo que puedia dar
> Y los bueyeros decieron que lo iban a repostar
>
> Pero como la sangre dentro las raices del Alamo
> La vida de ese novillo esta conectada a ti y yo
> Cuando llega la primavera el Enos no va tener ni una vaca
> Y nuestra vida que se cambia tanto, otra ves se retraca

Gente de Santa Rita no firma nada de ellos
En el nombre de Dios te van a sacar tu cuello
No son mala gente, pero piensan que ustedes necesitan
    salvacion
Pero las cosas necesarias por vida ya los tienes en su corazon

He Viewed the Town and Wept Over It

Luke 19:41

Nineteen fifty-five was the last good year. Ponce sold in 1926, but the devil did not come into Santa Rita until New Year's Eve, 1955. He was dressed in white, and the women came to him asking to dance. He had made himself into a big man. His left hand was ringed with gold. Only Nomio had shinier shoes. Everyone was there.

From a corner of the Rio Lounge you could hear pins falling at the end of the bowling lane. Each time a ball was hurled, the children would run to the end of the lane to replace the pins on the faded red dots. The children were the only ones who did not notice when the devil walked into El Rio Lounge. They did not see how the Schlitz bar light attached its neon redness to him and followed him as he walked toward the center of the room. They did not see their mothers turn or hear Apollonio when he missed a note on his crooked guitar. Nomio noticed the devil's shoes, followed them as he played his guitara de los dos cuernos. Many said that Rafael Trujillo did not notice the devil because he was leaning into his piano, his face inches from the keys, but Rafael noticed that the light shifted and

38

saw something red reflected in the keys of his treble hand.

It was the last good year and Malinche Santistevan-Matthews knew it. She hadn't left after school like she had planned. She only needed for a man like this one to take her from Santa Rita and its adobe buildings with tin roofs, from its dirt roads and cold winters. The man was light skinned but not like the bueyeros. Malinche Santistevan-Matthews was the first to ask him to dance. He was tall and her head rested on his thick chest. Her hair smelled of lilac and store-bought soap. His chest carried the scent of clothes hung out on a line, but deeper down Malinche Santistevan-Matthews believed he smelled of smoke, the clean kind that people walk into willingly. He smelled of burning aloe wood, but Malinche Santistevan-Matthews could not have known that.

The two guitar players were not afraid of him. Neither had a reason to be. They played and watched without fear as Malinche Santistevan-Matthews refused to let one of the bueyeros wives cut in. The song ended. Three pins echoed to the floor of the bowling lane. A little girl giggled at the poor shot and two boys raced each other to collect the three pins and place them on their marks.

The man danced well, smooth as a leaf on moving water. All the men stood at the bar, each posturing, each afraid of the man in the white suit. One of them mumbled that they could all take him. He motioned for the men to grab their bottles. The man in the perfectly white suit, even through Rafael's piano and the tumbling bowling pins heard him and looked over from the dance floor. All the men turned from his stare as their wives lined up to dance.

Perhaps he would have been fine, dancing all night, a different woman every song, but the devil is like bad water and will pour in through the weakest spots. He should never have danced with Malinche Santistevan-Matthews twice.

The mark of a brave man is that he is ultimately afraid. The difference between the brave man and those standing at the edge of the dance floor was that Aresando Vargas was also angry. His body was the place where two rivers meet, the place where two waters meet and swirl. His body was two rivers that rose where they met and then flowed away with only one name. The greater water always kept its name.

The man with the shiny shoes and the white suit took Malinche Santistevan-Matthews into a corner where only the Schlitz beer light followed. He had made his choice. The red light blinked around and danced with them. Malinche Santistevan-Matthews looked up and the man began to lean in. The devil knew that Aresando was coming, but the man in the white suit did not care. The devil outweighed him by fifty pounds. The devil leaned into Malinche Santistevan-Matthews, someone rolled a strike, Rafael Trujillo let his hands go and disappeared into the piano's voice, Apollonio and Nomio stopped playing; there was something furious on the piano, the sound of Aresando's feet on the oak floor running toward the red light. Otherwise, the night was quiet as everyone watched.

Behind El Rio Lounge there was a bare spot at the center of a ring of cottonwoods. The ground was frozen and the huge man had taken off his coat. The people of Santa Rita circled both of them. Aresando looked small, the red light still followed the man in white. He cast a shadow that was not his form but no one noticed because among the trees he looked bigger than before. Samuel yelled out to his son.

"His ring. Don't let him hit you with his ring."

The man's left hand glittered gold, but on the smallest finger of his right hand he wore one ring, a large red stone bulged from the gold band. Aresando knew the man in the white suit would come with his left hand first, but it was the right hand that he watched.

The devil had not spoken since he arrived, but when he did, the December air smelled of dead cats.

"You're mine," he growled.

It was the last good year. Everyone was gathered there on the last night of 1955. The devil had meant that they, all of them, were his, but no one knew that then. They did not know he meant to take something that had taken more than two hundred years to build. The devil comes like bad water through the oldest and weakest parts of a place.

It's true what they said. Jesus did view Jerusalem and weep over it. It was an act of mercy before his own death. Every great place has tumbled. All people, sometime in their history, have been conquered. It was the last good year.

No one blamed Aresando. He had come home from the war two years earlier, crazy and full of death. They only remembered that he was the only one who was not afraid.

Jesus viewed the town on that last night of 1955. He wept over Santa Rita. He did not weep to save the town or to cleanse the devil's bad water. Even the great lake city of the Aztecs fell, but only the place died. The people lived and so too did memory. The devil's intent was not to kill Aresando because he could not. So the devil seeped like water into the cracks of things. Things rot from the inside out. Much ended on that night.

Jesus ascended after they stripped him and cast lots for his belongings. Santa Rita would not be saved until she too had been stripped, her possessions divided. That is how things had always been.

The devil was in things, and Jesus wept over the town so that its loss would be the people's salvation.

A Reed Being Tossed by the Wind

Luke 7:24

Nomio first left for the high camps when he was ten. He worked with Carillo, the best of the herders. Years later, Carillo would be kicked by a horse, it was the blow that would end his life.

All was not tragedy, though. Blue Lake was deep and cold, the water glassing to a rock cliff; in the center of the glassy water there was an island with stunted pine growing. From the lake El Rito Azul spun cold through a great mountain meadow and then dropped south through a canyon before losing its name and turning east with the ancient river that cut the canyon where Santa Rita bloomed. The nights were cold and in the deep trees there were bears crying into the dark. The bears sounded human, a deep cry that comes from loss. In time the big bears would disappear from this place. There is no knowing like that of your demise, and perhaps those great hump-backed bears knew it then and sang their end into the pines and alpine meadows. In time the sheep would disappear from this place, too. Unlike the bears, the sheep would not be mourned, but a few would remember them, how they emerged like ghosts from the tree fog of an early morning, the way they scattered themselves across the meadow and up the ladera. Old memories would emerge of Carillo and his sombrero lifted above his gray head. In the green distance of those memories, at the edge of the meadow, Carillo's dog would look back. He loved that dog, and the pinto dog, in its way, returned the affection, watching its master for the waving of his hat. It was by that waving that he would move the sheep wherever Carillo wanted them. Carillo was the one who taught Nomio how to take the world in. Both of them pointed with all their fingers, there was always too much to see. The sheep scattered across the meadow and up the hillside where everything moved toward the horizon and became the memory that both men would hold forever.

There is no way of knowing the mountains and the cold deep lakes. Each high place has its own spirit that was born into it, but there is something more to a place, what the human brings to it. This thing is not the piano that was loaded on the back of a wagon and delivered to Blue Lake behind six giant horses. It isn't the cabin of wood, mud and stone chimney that was built on the west side of the lake, opposite the reflecting cliff. The piano would be tossed into the lake by some drunken hunters from Kansas. They wanted to see if it would float. It did not. The following summer when the herders returned, they knew what had happened. Everything is harsher and more beautiful up high. The piano was crafted in New York City by a father and son. The date etched above the keys gave the year. By giving it that birth, the two piano makers must have anticipated its death, they sought to mark its existence. 1896, No. 7 etched into brass was the piano's name and for a time it played opposite the crying bears, not as beautifully or as mournfully but drifting the same song into the night.

This thing that Nomio had always sought to identify was more than memory. The cabin burned, the chimney remained, and he rarely thought of either. Even the piano is secondary. He always tried to remember the song, but that fell too because Nomio knew the singer was the important thing. He observed that the human voice, if the song was right and it was sung beneath a living tree, that the sound of that voice would live as long as that tree. We all need a tree to shelter us, to preserve us.

Nomio would look out across the great meadow and in the green wind-tossed reeds along El Rito Azul he would see his friend Carillo who loved his dog because that was all he had. He would see that autumn when the herd was almost home, the road clogged with sheep, and he would see the canela horse Carillo rode, in the green reeds he saw the dog's anticipation as the sombrero came into Carillo's hand. The road was clogged with sheep and the gringo from Texas could not get through with his camper. Carillo lifted his hat and pointed straight ahead, and the dog knew to clear the road. The Texan rushed through and did not pause after he ran over the pinto dog. Carillo yelled at them but they did not stop. From his scabbard the .30-.30 came up to his left shoulder and he emptied it into the Texan's truck and camper. Nomio was twelve the year that happened, his second year with Carillo, his last. No one died. The Texan took a ricochet in the shoulder and his wife got broken glass in her eyes. Carillo was already old by then, but he was sent to prison for five years. He got out and never worked up high again. It was a July when the horse kicked him as he was loading her into a truck. Nomio was with the herd, alone, somewhere near Los Brazos on his way to Blue Lake. He found out about his friend's death a month later.

He was ten years old when he met Carillo, twelve the

year the dog died, and forty-three years later as he watched the reeds along El Rito Azul being tossed by the wind, it came to him that it only takes one reed of grass to remember your life.

We Played the Flute For You
But You Did Not Dance

Luke 7:31

Pelayo had been gone since 1910, when he'd told Adelaida he would be back soon, that he was going for seed to plant grain. At first he had meant to come home, had actually gone off for barley seed. He reached the mill where he used to come with his father. He remembered those days. The horses turned and turned. The grain became flour, and as they turned Pelayo remembered that novillo, the day the bueyeros came. By spring his father had butchered the entire herd. The bueyeros had their own animals, none of them were worth eating. The trail from Mississippi had left them all hollow and hungrier than the bueyeros. The bueyeros fed their animals with his father's hay that winter. They promised to repay him for his kindness. By spring his father's cows were gone and the bueyeros had saved his soul for their version of the same God. His father had no animals, the bueyeros had over a hundred, now fat, but no place to feed them. Enos' meadows were thick and low, cut by the river of stone, the grass thickest in the shade of the ancient cottonwoods. In exchange for his meadows, the bueyeros left

Pelayo's father with a canvas tent and the small plot beneath a crooked cottonwood, the home Pelayo was leaving.

Enos had died the year before, a runaway wagon, horses that had been spooked by a boy hunting along the road; a gunshot got them running. Nomio was seven, riding with his abuelito, neither of them strong enough to pull the horses in. Enos saved what he could before the wagon smashed into the cottonwood where the road turned at the edge of what used to be his meadow, the cottonwood where the steer had hung years before. Enos threw Nomio from the wagon into the grass and the boy was not hurt. He tried to jump himself but was too late. The horses had made the turn and the wagon did not go with them. He jumped and rolled toward the cottonwood but the wagon followed. They had buried Pelayo's father in the bueyero's cemetery and there was someone, a bueyero, responsible for praying him into heaven.

Pelayo watched the horses turning, knew that with one sack of barley he could plant all that was left him and still not use all the grain. Had he known about the two youngest he would have turned around, but he did not. He rode south across the llano toward the still pulsing star his father had watched. For all he knew, the star was dead. He told himself that the star was dead as he rode that night. The pulsing star was dead and only its light remained, pulling him away.

The devil did not kiss her, but afterward the men were prone to leaving, disappearing, really. Afterward, the wind began and the snow melted with it, like it had always done, but this time it did not stop. Some say it was the wind that drove the men away, made them crazy. Everything blew away it seemed. Pelayo had been the first and the men knew of him, how he kept riding and did not return. He had died the year before in a good bed. Noah had built his ark, but the men of Santa Rita had no such vessel with which to weather the wind and the water that rose with it.

There among the dust and swirling husks of men, the women stood. It's not a secret; the women were stone, and the wind did not enter.

Adelaida Arroyo married Pelayo in 1894. By the time he left for seed, she had five children and his last name. Nomio was her oldest. After his father left, Nomio would leave their adobe early in the mornings and walk the train tracks just up the dirt road from the adobe house. Along the tracks he would pick up pieces of coal that had spilled over the night before as the train rocked through Santa Rita on its way over the San Juans. When there was need for wood, he would offer to chop it for his mother, but mostly Adelaida chopped it herself. Nomio was nine. His mother did everything and he helped her as best he could, with his bits of coal, opening gates, sending water into the ditches. It was June when the baby and the other boy became sick. Adelaida prayed the girl into heaven and the boy back to health. When the fevers and the funeral passed, there was nothing left to eat. Nomio had kept the wood box full, the fields wet, but there was nothing for the wood to cook and it would be autumn before the beans and potatoes would come in.

The girl who died was almost two and the boy who lived turned one while the fever was still with him. Mana Virginia came and the two women began to cut potatoes into thin slices. The potatoes stained their hands white, as if they were made of salt. The women would take the slices, dip them in vinegar and one by one place them like communion on the hot skin of the two children. There was no cure for the fever, no ice left in the soterrano; the potatoes held the vinegar and the vinegar cooled the skin. The potatoes would turn black and the women would begin again. Virginia, in those two weeks, delivered six babies and after each one she would return to Adelaida's house and the two women would work far into the night. Neither slept. Finally, there were no more potatoes to slice or fry. There was no meat.

The girl died before dawn of the twelfth day. Nomio rose early, his mother was praying, and the small house held her voice in the quiet blue dark before dawn. The birds began singing. There were no clocks. The days were already long and the sun was coming when the girl died wrapped in her mother's prayers and birdsong. Her name was Sebastiana.

Adelaida's house was empty and abandoned in 1956 when all the other men began leaving. One day the wind began. They had expected it; the wind always came. They went to bed with the wind rattling their tin roofs. In the morning one man would return to his home beaten to death, his body stiff and tied to a pale horse. They would lose everything in that wind. They had expected the wind to melt the snow and for the water to rise. They could not have known they would melt and wash away, too.

When all the money was gone the men began to sell to each other and to the bueyeros. When the land was gone and the new fences erected, the bottles appeared beneath them. In the cantina there was music. The songs were about them and their life, but too much had changed. No one danced.

Cassiano Casias was the worst fisherman in the world. He had only taken up fishing lately. His wife, at first, did not question him. The other men had begun to drink and fight after the man in the white suit had fought Aresando. Cassiano, however, chose to fish and this was perfectly fine with Rosa. She never understood why he dressed up to go fishing, his clothes perfectly ironed, a tie, even his good shoes. He always came home empty handed. Rosa would put the puela on the stove every afternoon as he left, just in case, but there were never any fish, never any moss hanging from his hook or mud on his good shoes. She suspected it almost immediately, but she didn't know until she saw some boys follow Cassiano to the river. There were four of them, Blaesilla's children. They had lost their father in an accident at the lumber mill in Costilla. He was unloading a wagon when the lumber shifted and fell on him. He did not die immediately. He rode home, ate dinner and went to bed forever. Blaesilla had told him to call on Mana Virginia, but he said he would be fine, that only his leg hurt. The youngest of the four boys, Patricio, was a month old then. As Rosa watched her husband walk toward the river, the boys would duck behind trees and fall into the grass like dead birds every time Cassiano seemed to look back, all except Patricio who was lagging behind his older brothers, following only because that was what he had been told to do. The boy seemed more interested in grasshoppers, but he kept behind the other three, steadily losing ground until all of them were out of sight.

The three older boys came back before Cassiano. They were laughing and making motions with their hips, their faces contorted like treetops pushed by a hard wind. Later, Patricio came out of the trees carrying one of Cassiano's shoes. He walked slowly, his focus completely on the shoe, his small hand over its opening. Rosa thought that maybe her husband had fallen in. She was surprised that she did not feel sad about this. She walked across the vegita and met Patricio near the acequia.

"Donde? Como?" She pointed at the shoe.

Patricio said he found it by the river where the naked man and his tia Theodata were fighting in the grass. Rosa grabbed the shoe from Patricio. He looked more sad than scared. A gray brown chapulin, the kind that can fly, hopped from the shoe onto Rosa's apron. Patricio thought about reaching for it, but Rosa had already begun to walk toward the river to confront the world's worst fisherman. She took off her apron and threw it over a cedar fence post. It stayed there for years, slowly evaporating. Sometime between taking off the apron and reaching the river, she turned around and went back to the house. She placed Cassiano's shoe on the cold stove next to the unused puela. Then she walked out and never went back.

It was probably wrong to say that the women were like stone. Stone does not live well, it waits for the earth to consume it or the spring river to tumble it away. The women were not stone. They were something more than that, much more. They were like dancing, each paced differently but always moving with a rhythm that even good men cannot find. Those women were like dance, and in all the dust of men leaving, drinking too much, fishing poorly and wind blowing, they made their own music which they moved to.

All the men had promised their wives cedar trunks; it was the romantic thing to do in those days, protect the women's nice things from the dust and moths. The women in that time were powerful, and their daughters inherited those cedar trunks, heavy and overflowing with books.

Mark Well How the Lilies Grow

Dear Nonnatusia,

All those kids, all of us kids in one classroom. Do you remember how Mrs. Trujillo had us teach the little kids to read? You were always the smartest, but do you remember that girl who no one could teach to read. Her mom sent her to school with the nuns and she came back with syllables missing from her name. She still couldn't read. I remember her always jumping on the big rock by the swings. She would jump up there and sing, or at least pretend to sing. She's not like that now. She is pretty holy. I saw her at church, she sat two pews behind you and to the left. Your blue dress sure was beautiful. My uncle Nomio told me there is a lake as blue as your dress and that is why I'm writing. I won't be going back to school after the rodeo, like we always do. I'm not even going to the rodeo. I'll be up high with my tio looking after the sheep. I'm gonna carve your initials into a tree. I promise I won't change like that girl that used to jump on the rock. My uncle Nomio said his friend Apollonio was singing about our school closing. That the big kids wouldn't be able to go there anymore. Samuel and Elle from up the road said the same thing. If Mana Virginia says it, then for sure for sure. Maybe you already heard all this. I'm only telling you so that they don't take syllables from you too. All the kids from that school talk funny. They sound like rocks on tin. I love your name, all the vowels and it can have four or five syllables, depending on how you hear things. I hear five. Nonnatusia, I could say that all day. I hope you don't think I'm a little off or anything.

I'll be back in October, before the first snow. My tio Nomio says I will be a man by then. So I guess that means I'll have money and I'll be able to visit you. I'll carve your initials in a tree and I'll bring you something from up high. My tio says everything is prettier up there so it shouldn't be hard to find something nice, even though I know the prettiest things are down here wearing blue. Take care.

Affectionately,

Ramon

p.s. turns out that lion from the last letter was actually a panther. That's what Mrs. Trujillo told me. Maybe she'll go teach at the other school. She won't let the nuns lose syllables and change names.

Adios, Again

With Affection,

Ramon

This Man of Another Nation

Luke 17:18

She prayed like a brief rain on a still lake, randomly with too many prayers to count, none of them making a difference. In her bedroom, hanging over the only mirror in the house, there was a picture of the ascension. In it, Jesus was flying and wrapped in light, arms outstretched, palms turned up. His body formed the Y of the word yes. That is what Elle believed.

There were four days in June, the twenty-second was the last of them, when the sun would come through the bedroom window. In the early rising of the sun on those days the light would reflect off the picture of Jesus and cast a small prism of rainbow on the opposite wall. She prayed like rain, brief rain on a still lake, and those four days of morning light were her only proof of God. It was enough.

Dear Lord, let my son cry...water is the only thing that cleans...dear Lord let me die before Samuel so I'm not alone...dear Lord I'm sorry for my sins...look after Samuel and Aresando keep them in your care...dear Lord thank You for all that you do for me...look after Samuel's family and mine too...take care of my abuelitas and abuelitos in heaven, my tio who always smiled, my tias and all the muertos...look after my dog Rover and that charlais cow that fought the six coyotes away from her beserro, thank you for letting me see that when I was a girl so I could understand what a mother is supposed to be...please say hello to your own mother and have her watch over us too...thank you for the rain...I'm sorry I spoke poorly of people and gossiped what the crickets said...thank you for my gift... look after Adelaida who is alone and hungry...take care of Pelayo too, you must have your reasons for making him leave...I'm sorry I questioned you just now, but so much is happening...pray...well you don't have to pray I do...look after Arabal Fernandez who was found dead yesterday... pray...I mean forgive those men who beat him and tied him to his horse...thank you for directing the horse home so his family could know...please don't let Malinche Santistevan-Matthews make my boy crazy...she is back, living in town with someone she brought from the city...I'm sure you already know that since you directed it...forgive me Lord for not liking her and not trusting that man, his hands scare me, he has money and does not work...forgive me for judging that is yours and your father's work...tell him hello too...thank You Lord for all that you do and for protecting us...look after our town, it needs you. Amen.

The prism of rainbow lasted only a minute or two, longer on the first day than on the fourth, and when it was gone she would rise from her stinging knees, the picture of Jesus now completely flooded in light, and cross herself before moving toward the kitchen and the coffee Samuel had already poured.

"Did you pray for me?"

"I don't remember," she joked.

"That girl is back."

"I know. I prayed about that."

"Did you pray for that cow?" He smiled and winked.

"You know I did. She was beautiful. I didn't really pray for her. I gave thanks."

"What if she would have let those coyotes eat her calf?"

"She wouldn't have. She was a mother."

"But they chewed off its ear. What kind of mother…"

She cut him off and scolded him with her eyes. He already knew the story, but he liked to make her mad. Both of them were already old. This was their substitute for passion.

"They came at night, during the night as the beserro was being born. They chewed its ear off while it was being born, la charlais was down on the ground, in labor, but the ear is all they got."

"Sounds like they got you too. You're still mad."

"You wouldn't understand."

"I know, what it's like to be a mother."

"That worthless bull didn't help her fight off those coyotes. Ese toro didn't kill two of those coyotes. You know what that bull did?"

"Watched like a dumb bull?"

"You're hopeless. Drink your coffee and shut up."

"Do you think Aresando will find out about her man?"

"Drink your coffee, I'm thinking."

"Thinking like that cow how you are going to save your baby?"

He knew he shouldn't have even as he was saying it. He knew immediately what was coming but his joke was heavy in the room and he could not bring it back.

"What do you do? Nada. Let him go to that war, let him fight that man, that ugly coyote of a man who almost killed him, and for what, esa green eyes. You should protect your son, not sit there like a dumb bull. Cabron toro, that's what you are."

Samuel knew to keep quiet but he could not.

"I couldn't stop him. He sighed. And that guy for New Years, it was not right. Aresando gave what he got. That guy won't come around no more. My boy fought like a man. Stood up when no one would."

"That man is back."

"Como?"

"He just looks different. Everything else is the same. I recognized his ring."

If Even the Salt Loses Its Strength

Luke 14:34

Ramon Fernandez was in the half-light of the bosque where the trees cast their thin shadows away from the afternoon sun. Nonnatusia's name crossed his lips. The white aspen and the sombra they cast reminded him of home, of Rafael Trujillo and his piano. He missed the music. He missed Nonnatusia. The sheep began to drift into the piano keys Ramon had imagined; they moved silently into the sombra to escape the heat. Ramon Fernandez did not wear a watch, but the train's whistle would come soon, three lonely blasts into the mountain air, exhaling its black breath as it rolled toward the water tower. Nomio would be waiting for the train there, waiting to collect bags of salt for the sheep. Ramon Fernandez was alone but off to his left he could hear one of the herders moving his sheep toward camp, the man's voice echoed up the canyon and hung in the air for awhile, and then the breeze would take it. There were seven bands of sheep up high that year. Ramon and Nomio looked after the smallest of them. Sometime before the trees began their migration to gold, all the herders would drive their sheep to the corral beside the water tank. From there the lambs would be counted and loaded on the train, a receipt handed to each herder, a piece of paper signed by Ambrose Benedict-Matthews that promised to pay them the going rate upon his return from the sales in Denver.

The sheep were lying in the shadows, their lambs by their side. The train whistled three times, the aspen shifted their leaves in a slight breeze, green gray green. Beneath Ramon the grass was cool, his hat covered his face in sombra, he looked older after fourteen years with the herd, his jaw set, his lips expressionless. The echoes of the herder in the canyon reached him again, they seemed lonelier than the train's whistle. He had learned many things from his tio, learned that Jesus was not wrong to call himself a shepherd and the people his flock. There in the sombra of the bosque he saw Rafael's piano, he saw his tia Adelaida's abandoned house beneath a bent cottonwood, Nonnatusia standing in a field of clover and brome, lirios purpling all around her, he saw the ditches rising and the water spilling into the fields, he saw Mana Virginia walking in the dusk along the river, her soft hands picking mint, he saw his abuelita making tortillas, the flour cupped in her hands and then spilling into a wooden bowl, in the shadows and in the sheep that had entered the shadow he saw the people of Santa Rita. He could not have known it then, no one did. Jesus was a shepherd who sought the one while the ninety-nine remained in the wilderness. He could not have known that the one had already parted from the herd and that Jesus had already brought it back to the flock. He could not have known that Ambrose Benedict-Matthews would take the lambs before autumn and never return, could not have known that his father had been beaten and tied to his horse. The news would reach him later when Nomio returned with the two hundred pounds of salt. No one knew Santa Rita was lost, that of the seven herds up high only one would ever return. They could not have known that the land they were selling to each other belonged to none of them, could not have known that Arabal Fernandez had found three men from a lumber outfit putting up a fence on what he thought was his land. He had gone for his gun, a pistol on his right side, but one of the three threw his hat toward the horse and spooked her, his first and only shot sailing high. The sheep rested in the shade, safe in their numbers and the eye of Ramon Fernandez, none of them knowing that they would disappear and take Santa Rita with them. The walls would remain, the people would remain, but Santa Rita would fade. It may have been the devil, already the people were selling land to the bueyeros, they were counting the water now, fences were going up, word had not reached him yet that his father's horse had found its way home. There in the bosque he could hear the echoes roll up the canyon, see his own herd in front of him, scattered loosely in the aspen. The devil's water had risen that year washing away a maze of ink signed almost a hundred years earlier when America had come to the people of Santa Rita. The people were like the borregas that Ramon Fernandez looked after, none of them knowing they had been left alone since 1926 when Ponce Santistevan-Matthews had sold a small piece of land to his father in law. When America came to the people in 1848, they had all been promised their land, the land that had been theirs since 1598 when they had stolen it away from the Indios and agreed to share it amongst themselves. Communidad, they prospered without money and never missed what they did not have. Even the great lake city of the Aztecs was torn down by the Spanish, the stone blocks of the pyramids and the temples thrown into the lake. Santa Rita had once been part of New Spain and then

Mexico. Ponce's grandfather had been governor, distributor of the land grants. The Americans knew nothing of communidad; there could only be one owner and without knowing it Ponce was the owner. He had always told Malinche that she was a descendant of royalty; that was all he had cared about. Everything else had disappeared from his memory, but the paper remained. He signed away all 600,000 acres to Ambrose Benedict-Matthews and never even knew it was his to sell. All that was left of them were the small squares of land where their homes stood. Maybe it was the devil that whispered it to Ambrose Benedict-Matthews, maybe on one of his trips to Denver he tried to file his title for his eight hundred acres and realized that he was richer than he imagined. When he began selling was not completely known to the people of Santa Rita, but when the three men from the lumber company tied Arabal Fernandez to his horse, everything changed. Ambrose Benedict-Matthews had always wanted to go somewhere great, somewhere west, maybe San Francisco. He could have left that night, but he wanted more and had sent word with the train that the prices were high and they should sell. He would write them their paper receipts like he had always done and never return.

The death of Arabal Fernandez would save Nomio's herd. The two men would attend the funeral and miss the train that sent everything north.

Ramon Fernandez sat watching his herd and did not know any of this. He only knew that Jesus had been a shepherd and that when the flock was lost he would save them from the wilderness. Once one sheep leaves the others follow. Every herder knew this. As he sat there, Nonnatusia's name crossed his lips again, the train whistled its departure from far away and the borregero in the canyon had finally reached his camp and fallen silent.

In the trees above Ramon there were two birds singing to each other in the aspen and the sun caught the trees
golden. The birds were proof that Nonnatusia loved him.
He could not have known what Nomio would deliver. He
only knew that Nomio was coming with salt, not that everything had already wandered off like a single sheep into the
wilderness and that Jesus had already saved it without anyone knowing.

Joy Arises

Luke 15:10

Aresando stood in the saddle of his Indian, arms outstretched. He was made of wind. Two years removed from the war, he was brave and crazy and everyone came to watch him ride down the dirt roads, dust trailing behind into the eyes of those watching until they could not see him. They wondered, there in the dust of the passing motorcycle, if they had really seen him, arms outstretched, caught in the sunlight, the machine rumbling beneath him. He was beautiful there in the summer light. Water from the fields pooled by the roadside and he was reflected there. Blaesilla, the widow, came with her four kids to watch him, the infant Patricio in her arms, and he was reflected in her eyes too. The sun was thick, the lirios high and the dust from his passing settled softly on everyone and everything. The people followed him, even the bueyeros, to the vegita by the river.

The vega belonged to Juan de Jesus Sanchez, the best farmer in Santa Rita. It was cut short, weeks ahead of the other farmers. The hay, piled in a semi-circle, formed the outfield fence. Dionicio Sandoval had closed the cantina, he was in left field, closest to the road. The smell of the cut hay was with him and he was remembering a woman, how he took her face into his hands and kissed her, he was remembering the way they fell into the clover and mint along the river. In his memory he had reached the smooth field of her belly when Aresando's motorcycle broke his dream memory. Aresando was facing west, the motorcycle rolled east as he used his hands to steady himself as he spun and spun in the saddle, east west east. Dionicio had forgotten his dream memory; he watched as the crazy man moved up the motorcycle to sit on the handlebars, his feet held together above the spinning wheel. The Indian slowed and the dust behind it fell flat as linen dropped over a line, hanging there as Aresando jumped off the still moving bike and ran beside it, slowly coaxing it to a stop beneath the cottonwoods behind home plate.

Apollonio was ancient so he played first base. Aresando, who was crazy, was behind the plate. Edimundo Trujillo would pitch. He was the youngest one on the team, the tallest and thinnest. He, too, in the summer sun at the heart of the field, was beautiful. His leg kicked high, the ball held close against his chest, he didn't wear a hat, he looked directly into the sun, felt it briefly on his eyelids and lips, the scent of his leather glove rising into his nostrils, his hands separating, his right arm cocking at the wrist and elbow, the long muscles of his shoulder contracting, his left leg falling toward the ground, planting itself in the short grass, his hips turning toward the plate, his body coming square as his right arm whipped across his body, wrist snapping, the ball invisible in the rising waves of heat; the loud crack of it meeting Aresando's glove was the most perfect of sounds.

Nomio was at second base, still the swiftest of all the men, his beautiful shoes collected no dust. Samuel, who could read the other team's signs by way of the crickets, was managing. He sat along the first base line, his body resting on a plank of cedar spanning across three blocks of pino taken from Jose Francisco Salazar's woodpile. Jose Francisco played shortstop and hit sixth, right behind Sebastiano Avila, the centerfielder. Juan de Jesus Sanchez, the owner of the field and best farmer in Santa Rita was in right field, closest to his adobe house. His grandson, Alfonzo, would be at third and bat third because he always made contact.

1955 was the last good year and this was the greenest time of that year. The bueyeros had fielded a team, most of them played at the college sixty miles up the road. They wore uniforms, white with green lettering across the chest. They called themselves the Zion Zephyrs.

When the Zion Zephyrs saw the field and the men in it, they refused to play, noting that the pitcher had no hat, the second baseman wore shiny boots, the first baseman was clearly over ninety years old and none of them had uniforms. The Zion Zephyrs were undefeated, too good to be brought to this level. They refused to take the field to lead off the first. It just wasn't proper, a travesty to the game they called it.

Apollonio called in the team and asked them to empty their pockets. There was ninety-two dollars and eighteen cents among them, the majority coming from Nomio, who had just sold two lambs. They sent Jose Francisco Salazar with the money. Of the nine, he was the most diplomatic. Jose Francisco at first thought to pay the bueyeros, ten dollars an inning with the remainder going to an umpire of their choosing. By the time he reached the bueyeros, all of them over six feet tall and burning to a bright red along the unshaded third base line, he had decided a bet was more the way to go.

"Ninety-two eighteen," he said, the money folded and stacked in his right hand. "Bet you guys. All of it. Even money."

The bueyeros didn't have any money; all of it had been spent on their uniforms and green hats with a white Z sewn into the crown.

"No bet there Jose. We don't gamble." It was Chance Crowsen, their cleanup hitter, six-foot-six and 280 pounds, right-handed and always ahead of the pitch; everything went to left field with Chance Crowsen .

"You don't play. You don't gamble. What do you guys do?" Jose Francisco, the diplomat, had hoped they would send over Crowsen. Jose Francisco was five-foot-seven and 163 pounds, tiny compared to the cleanup hitter. Nobody that big likes to be challenged by someone smaller than himself. "We'll spot you two runs plus the the $92.18."

"We don't gamble." He was less convincing this time.

Jose Francisco turned to his team. "They don't gamble."

From the shade of the trees there was laughter, the spectators pointing at the well dressed team.

"We'll play you, but not in this cow pasture. Come to the college and we'll play on a real field with fences, with chalk, with places for people to sit."

Jose Francisco Salazar turned back to face his team. "They want to be able to sit down."

Again the trees seemed to laugh. Samuel stood up and offered his plank to the bueyeros. He moved slowly as he reached beneath the cedar plank and lifted a tin bucket full of water and moved carefully toward the third base line.

Chance Crowsen was angry now, but Jose Francisco was not afraid.

Mana Virginia came out of the shade and walked toward the two men. She seemed ancient too, but she moved quickly and did not stumble.

"Jose Francisco, why don't you offer to play two games. One here and one on their field? Everyone is already here," she gestured toward the trees. "Besides, you men already have your white suits on."

"This ain't an official game, but we'll play, and not because the old lady or you asked, but because we came all this way, but this ain't no official game. You hear me?"

Jose Francisco thanked Mana Virginia and turned toward the eight waiting on the first base line. "It's official. This game is unofficial, but they'll play so long as we play them next week on their field."

Joy arises like a river in spring, a bird in the wind, a voice singing, a butterfly on a windmill, a baby's first breath, like a man standing on his Indian motorcycle, the first dawn you remember, grain coming bright green into spring, sheep blooming into a meadow, the first wall of your home, cedar smoke in winter, untraceable laughter, joy arises and brings everyone with it, it rises like morning prayers, a mother's wish for her child, it rises like summer in a canyon cut by ice, joy arises and the people come with like a sinner who finds salvation, a winter that finds love and no death, a year where nine men played in an open field, joy arises like a widow's wish for love, willows along the river, a fish beneath the willows, a third baseman's leap toward the line, it arises and the people will never forget it, it arises and keeps them, joy comes fast like a fastball rising, a bat swinging, and the perfect sound of ball meeting leather.

The bueyeros could not hit Edimundo. Chance Crowsen fouled off a pitch, one man hit one hard toward third, but he did not beat out the throw. The score did not matter to the people of Santa Rita. They knew they had won and the other team had two runs they had given them. None of the nine Santa Rita players had cars. Aresando had his motorcycle, the rest walked or caught rides the following weekend and on the manicured field of the bueyeros they unofficially won again. The games did not count because the men of Santa Rita did not have uniforms or a league they belonged to. The bueyeros finished the season an official 18 – 0. Their trophy reads Undefeated, League Champions, 1955. The trophy is gold and rests dust free in a display case, a picture of the Zion Zephyrs framed and autographed behind it. Only two of them are smiling. All of their eyes are knowing and without joy.

Mark Well How the Lilies Grow

Dear Nonnatusia,

I think of you constantly now. The sheep have made the llano their home and the stars are changing toward winter. Everything here is calm and quiet. My tio Nomio has gone home for a few weeks and left me with the herd. When he returns we will drive the sheep home together, and I will finally get to see you. I hope school went well for you. I learned a lot up high, but it is good to be down here with all the black rocks and sage. Maybe this is because I know I am closer to you now. On a good horse I could see you in less than two hours. My horse is good but she is nothing like my tio's palomina. She can sure walk. I don't think any horse could keep up with her.

We call this campadero 'el campo de los cerritos.' From the mesa behind your house you can see them. The big mountain was a volcano. I'm sure you know that, but I think these two little hills were too. From my camp you can look forever to the east, even see where the Rio Grande cuts the llano in two. I liked it up high, but this feels more like home.

The other herders sure like my tio. They come and check on me, point out the mojoneras they have placed on the hills. The mojoneras all catch the horizon, especially at dusk. They are supposed to help you get home when the night is coming or the snow is blowing. To the east and a little to the north the mojoneras lead to a place that doesn't exist anymore. My tio said there was a lake there and on the hillside you can see the old acequias like scars. I looked at my tio's map and the lake is marked, still blue and everything, but there is no water. The houses there are made of the same rock as the mojoneras, stacked better and held together with white mortar, but they are the same rocks, full of holes where they cooled too fast or too slow, I can't remember. Anyway, the rocks are black but they have holes like a pancake before you flip it. The people just left. The wagons and plows are still in the straight fields, but nothing grows there. My tio said all the water from that lake up on the hill got sold. Hard to believe you can sell water. This is probably boring you. I'm sorry. I just miss home and I know all these rocks piled on the horizon are supposed to mean home. I just can't imagine a place disappearing, home disappearing, but those houses made of rock are proof.

I sure do miss you. I have something to give you when I get home. Something to ask you too. My first year up high was different than school but you can learn anywhere. My tio brings me books and I read by the light of the farolito. He brought me the book with the panther in it. That poem is sadder than I remember. Actually I only remembered it because of you. That panther in the cage, I wonder what he saw that made his eyes wild. What do panthers eat? The real sad part though is that the panther is wild and caged all at once. The feeling the panther gets, it goes through his heart and disappears. I wonder where it goes after the heart. Me, I keep my feelings in my heart. I recognize them too. Most of them are about you. I say your name to myself and maybe if someone were watching my eyes would be like the panther's, you know when it still thinks it has a chance and doesn't remember it is in a cage or out on the llano, close to home but not. Those poor empty houses and the panther's feeling. Everything disappears I guess. My tio says love doesn't and I'm hoping he is right, one more thing to learn.

Sorry this letter was sad. I guess the musicians play what they feel and I'm no different. Can't wait to see you. I'll show you how to skip rocks and I'm sure the music will change too. Sure miss you.

Love,

Ramon

p.s. —When it gets real dark and those three lined-up stars are in the north, planes come over the llano. I can hear them and see red lights blinking low to the ground. Sure would like to see one of those during the day, but not as much as I want to see you.

p.s.s.—After the planes leave, trucks come in the night and then turn towards town, not towards Santa Rita but towards where you go to school now. If they went toward home I'd take my horse down there and get a ride. Sorry I can't shut up.

Again, with Love

Ramon

I Came to Start a Fire on the Earth

Luke 12:49

There had been planes earlier, two of them. Ramon could not sleep, but Nonnatusia rested by his side, her breath was consistent as she rested beside Ramon. The tent was facing south to catch the sun during the day, but in the east the sun was beginning. The sheep stirred and a few of them were bleating into the madrugada. He wanted to sleep but could not. It wasn't the planes—he had grown used to them these past five years. Ramon could not sleep; he thought of his tio Nomio, the idea that memory is found in permanent things, the rocks, trees, campaderos, rivers, that memory was in things that humans return to. This was true, but Ramon could not sleep. He thought that memory sometimes comes to us in passing things, the way the light in winter could remind you of an abuelita, only a certain light, the way it slanted and aligned itself in a room, a light like that could bring memory too, passing but real. Outside the tent the air was heavy and calm, and later it would snow. In a few weeks Nonnatusia and he would go to their house along the river and he would make fires for her in the dawn. He would tend to the sheep, shear them with his tio, bring new lambs into the wet month of March. Nonnatusia would rise with him, he would watch as she braided her hair by the light of the growing fire, her hands would move in and out of the light. Her hands were like the memories he could not shake. He loved them all, but they were passing too quickly in and out of the November madrugada and he could not sleep.

A place never totally disappears. That is what Apollonio had said, but Ramon could only think of the rock houses beneath the dry lake. No one spoke of them. He had found their empty shells by accident, but Apollonio was right. He had found them and now that place was real and would come to him when it chose and this would keep the place. Santa Rita would never die like that place. He thought of his father, the pistol he inherited, the land he did not. Everything was gone now. Signed away by Ponce Santistevan-Matthews to his father-in-law. Not everyone lost their land. A few had managed to pay taxes. How they knew of such things Ramon could only guess, but he assumed that somehow they had heard that the only way to own land was to pay for it and then, after it was yours, continue to pay. His father had not known such things. The mountain where he was killed had been in Ramon's family since the second arrival of the Spanish. It had been in their family for over two centuries, but it disappeared and was coming to him now in the memory of his father.

Nonnatusia turned on her side, her back was to him now, but the sun was coming in under the flaps of the tent. The light was on her hair. He loved her like rivers of time. He thought of his abuelita and then he loved Nonnatusia like bread loves salt. He loved her completely and the sun on her black hair was orange and red. He began thinking of Juan de Jesus Sanchez and his white International, how they had tied the barandales to the flat bed of the truck and driven,

Juan, Nomio, and Ramon, to Montrose for peaches. The truck was geared low and it took them all day. They made camp in the grass along the road and drank water from a glass jug. His tio played his guitara de los dos cuernos and all of them sang. It was dusk, the light was like this but everything was louder. The next morning they had risen and gone to the orchards and bought the peaches straight from the field. They loaded over a hundred bushels and finished their work by sharing a peach. Juan de Jesus Sanchez had cut the peach and placed the pit on his dashboard to dry. The peach was still firm, but the meat of it was sweet and dripped from Ramon's lips onto his cheek. It was the light on Nonnatusia's hair that brought the memory to him, how they drove back to Santa Rita and shared the load with everyone. No one paid, they brought what they had, Salustiano brought them a load of wood and left with five bushels, Apollonio wrote a song about the men and left with one bushel, Mana Virginia left with three bushels on credit for seeing them through any illness that might come, Blaesilla brought trout her boys had caught, but Juan de Jesus Sanchez would not take them. He told her he didn't like fish, but really he knew the widow was without much. He gave her five bushels and only asked that when summer came her boys help him in his fields. He was the best farmer in Santa Rita, the boys would learn from him and Blaesilla took the peaches and gave her word. She handed each of her boys a piece of fruit and they all turned to thank Juan Sanchez. The boys were happy and Ramon remembered that too. Everyone came, everyone left with fruit and there was no money exchanged. Maybe Santa Rita would not disappear, but Ramon knew that the communidad of that day and all the days that preceded it would. He thought of waking Nonnatusia and telling her everything he was thinking. She was wrapped in red blankets, she rested on two zaleas, the wool still thick on them. Her body was as soft as rain pooled in a fallen leaf. He loved her and let her sleep.

In the hour before the sheep rose from the rodeo and begin to move east into the white sage of the llano, Ramon slept. Nonnatusia was next to him and the last thing he remembered before his dream was her body and its warmth. The dream was made of smoke and came to him the way the waking memories did. He dreamt of Salustiano who traded the wood for the peaches.

Salustiano is chopping wood Salustiano is chopping wood Salustiano is chopping wood he is made of wood, he is made of wood, he smells of pino, his blood is sap and smells sweet, Salustiano is made of wood, his eyes are piñon, in the cold morning Salustiano's lips are made of aspen, Salustiano is chopping wood, he is made of wood, his hands are the color of cedar, his hands are cedar, he knows the wood, he is made of it, his hands are cedar, his ax is ash and steel, his body does not stop, he is made of wood, his body moves like trees in the wind, his body bends between gusts, his ax and the sound it makes, it is the sound of trees breaking from the earth, the sound of trees in their last moment of stand-ing, he is wood, all the parts of him are made of these trees, his eyes are brown and hard, they are piñon, Salustiano is chopping wood, all of Santa Rita, all of Santa Rita in the still of winter night, all of Santa Rita when the people step from their homes, all of Santa Rita smells sweet, Santa Rita smells of wood smoke, Salustiano is made of smoke, the stars are beyond the smoke, they are hazy in the smoke, Salustiano is made of stars, he is made of wood, he knows its weakness, the trees are taller than the church, the trees are taller than the mountain, the trees grow from the mountain and are taller than their mother, Salustiano made of wood knows its weakness, Salustiano made of wood keeps his ax sharp, he is trees higher than everything in Santa Rita, his body is closest to all earthly things, of all earthly things his body is closest to the stars, Salustiano is chopping wood, Salustiano is chopping wood, he knows its weakness, his body reaches for the stars, his name is stars, Salustiano is chopping wood, the knots and swirls and grain of the wood are a universe, he is made of wood and knows this, his body bends with the gusts, each piece of wood has seen the stars more clearly than us, his body is made of wood, his body burns, smoke from his body covers Santa Rita, the houses are warm, the winter night smells sweet and lingers with everyone, the sweet smell lingers with us even after we have left this place, his name is stars, his name is wood, his body is a gift made of wood.

Not A Stone Upon Stone

Luke 21:6

Malinche Santistevan-Matthews was destined to be lucky. She had green eyes. It was her God given right, at least that is what her father told her.

It's not true what they say; we are not made of bone and blood. Humans, all of us, are made of choices. Our life is made of them the way the houses of Santa Rita are made of adobes. We are born blood and bone, but from that point on our life is made of pieces we can't even recall. Malinche Santistevan-Matthews had always been told she was a descendant of royalty and that her green eyes were proof. She did not make this choice for herself, it was piled there by her father who built his daughter into a house that even she couldn't live in.

Not many people know this, but Malinche Santistevan-Matthews was not a bad person. She actually liked Santa Rita, the birds on the riverbank, the way Apollonio played his crooked guitar. She even remembered playing there when she was young. It wasn't so bad.

Malinche and Blaesilla, long ago when she was fourteen and still allowed to associate with Blaesilla, had found an abandoned fawn curled up in the tall meadow grass. The venadito wasn't sleeping; its eyes were open, just lying there the way its mother had left it. It had rained the night before. Everything was wet there in the deep grass, at the edge of the field, near the trees. The girls had gone there to pick flowers and hide from their parents. They hadn't done anything wrong. They just felt like hiding. Malinche had found the newborn deer. It had been licked clean, maybe even fed once, but there was no mother in sight. Neither girl knew what to do. Both thought of leaving it there and eventually the crows or coyotes would find it. It was Malinche Santistevan-Matthews who said they should go ask Mana Virginia what to do. The girls ran west toward Mana Virginia's house, a small adobe in the shade of apple trees, a small ditch running behind the house. The grass was tall and both girls still felt young. They couldn't run fast enough, each fell several times, each of them wondered if they knew where they had left the fawn.

When they got to Mana Virginia's house she was waiting for them. There was a she-goat tied to one of the apple trees, and Mana Virginia held a brown bottle in her right hand. The bottle was warm when Mana Virginia placed it in Malinche's hand; it was full of milk. In Mana Virginia's left hand there was a black rubber nipple. With a knife, she had cut two small gashes at the top of the nipple. They were barely visible, but she showed the two girls how the top would open when the nipple was squeezed. The two girls tried it, Malinche first, placing the teta between her thumb and finger she pinched the top and she said it opened the way a flower would. Blaesilla tried it too, but could not think of anything as creative as Malinche. She handed it back to Mana Virginia and only said it looked as though there was a cross cut into the top.

"Hurry, take this milk before it gets cold. The little venado will be hungry but it won't like this teta. One of you must put your finger in the venado's mouth. It will nurse and both of you will feel happy. You should take turns letting the little venado suck on your fingers. When you think the venado is ready you should put the teta in its mouth. The milk needs to be warm so don't spend all day letting it suck on your finger. It will drink after that. Let it finish. When you are done you come back here and get more milk, five times a day, once as the sun is going away, so the venadito will make it through the night."

"My dad has a goat. I can get milk from her."

"No Malinche, only my goat will do."

"But,"

"The venadito will get sick with goat's milk, after all it isn't a goat, now is it?"

"No."

"My goat is special, only milk from my goat will do. Do you understand?"

Both girls said they did and began running back toward the fawn. They did exactly as Mana Virginia told them and the little venado drank until the botella made hollow noises and the black nipple was sucked flat. They took the teta from the venadito and Blaesilla pinched the end of it. The air rushed back into the bottle and made a popping noise as the nipple regained its shape. They named the venadito Arturo and agreed to take turns feeding it. Since Malinche Santistevan-Matthews was a descendant of royalty and, therefore, more free, she would feed Arturo as night was falling on Santa Rita.

Malinche Santistevan-Matthews was not a bad person and for proof of this she didn't look toward her green eyes but toward that meadow and the venado that she and Blaesilla raised that summer. Arturo followed them everywhere.

Once, as Malinche and the bigger kids were waiting for the bus to take them to the nun's school, Arturo had even gone into the old schoolhouse. All the younger kids laughed, but Aresando had helped push Arturo out the back door and into the meadow behind the school. Eventually the venado grew up thinking it was a goat, following the herds up to the high country in the summers and returning home with them in autumn. Arturo was a doe, and never had a fawn of her own. She followed the herds for three years and didn't come down one October. Nomio told Malinche Santistevan-Matthews that Arturo went off into the trees one day with all the other goats but did not return with them. Malinche cried and that was what she remembered now.

Malinche's house in town had electricity but she had never grown accustomed to the light. She waited in the living room with only a small lamp illuminating half of her body, the rest of the house waited with her and reflected how she felt now and on that day when Arturo did not return with the herd. We are all made of choices and Malinche Santistevan-Matthews had always been told that hers were already written. She didn't love the man she shared a house with. He was rich, with two cars, a truck, electricity in the house, and money to buy Malinche anything she wanted. She sat there in the half dark of her body and thought of Arturo. She pondered the possibility that maybe that summer was the last time she was ever happy, the last time she would ever be happy. She said the year to herself, "1946," and realized she could not remember the ten years that had fallen between.

Malinche Santistevan-Matthews did not love her former pilot husband. She did not love his medals for bravery, she wasn't impressed that he had shot down fifteen planes during the war in Europe. She wasn't impressed or in love with the money he brought home from selling cars to people who really didn't need them. In truth, he had only sold two cars in the year since he and Malinche had moved to the town just north of Santa Rita. The money did not stop coming though and Malinche Santistevan-Matthews was so disinterested that she didn't even know it wasn't from cars. She had heard other people talking about his other business and assumed, happily, that it must be a mistress. He had been brave in the war. Some say he was braver than Aresando. Her husband had medals that he kept in the top drawer of his dresser, she had seen them once and remembered being impressed because she thought she had to be. She maybe even loved him once, but she doubted that now. Malinche Santistevan-Matthews was destined to be lucky and leave this place for her proper place in the world. That was the idea she was trained to be in love with. That was the choice that led her to Karl Varshant.

Karl Varshant was a war hero, not a big man, smaller than average really, much older than Malinche Santistevan-Matthews. Other than his money and the gold and ruby ring on his right hand he was indistinguishable.

Malinche's grandfather had run off with everyone's money and life's work before Karl had met Malinche, thus leaving a void in the business end of things in town. Karl Varshant had listened to the story from Malinche shortly after they met, how there were letters from Chicago and even one from San Francisco, but Karl knew that Ambrose Benedict-Matthews, overcome by guilt for what he had done, had killed himself in a train station in Denver, hanged himself in the bathroom using a fine leather belt. This is what Karl Varshant knew to be fact and what he kept from the wife he didn't love.

Karl Varshant was the first to come upon the body of

Ambrose Benedict-Matthews. Karl had seen so many dead bodies that the image of Ambrose Benedict-Matthews' swollen face and blue lips did not even register with him at the time. The two men had met many years before, between the wars, but it is unlikely that Ambrose would have recognized the man who was now looking through his belongings and pocketing the money from the lambs Ambrose had sold. Karl Varshant did not need the money, but he took it anyway. He didn't even bother to count it; he could tell by the weight of it in his hand that it was over fifty thousand dollars. The wallet had a picture of Malinche. The back of the picture was signed to her grandfather. It read "To Grandpa with Love, 6th grade." Karl left the body hanging and put Malinche's picture in his breast pocket. He didn't need the picture, he would remember her face, but he took it anyway as a memento. He would look for her later and then finish his business.

Malinche Santistevan-Matthews had seen the men of Santa Rita come to her husband for work. He hired them all and in exchange for his money they stayed in town, worked some and then disappeared into the bars until finally they didn't come out again. There were others to replace the missing. She thought again of her venadito, how that was the only living thing she was ever allowed to love that didn't have money. The bulb from the small lamp seemed to flicker in the dark living room. Malinche Santistevan-Matthews noticed the light change and thought of the kerosene lamps in her father's house, she thought of going home, but her father would not understand her choice. Perhaps everyone can blame their fathers for their failings, for the choices their fathers made. Malinche Santistevan-Matthews' father had built her a life that she couldn't live. For all the luck her green eyes had brought her, she only wanted to remember how she and Blaesilla had stumbled upon that venadito in the rain-wet grass that summer. She thought of Aresando helping her push it from the schoolhouse, the way it had sucked on her fingers, the way she tested the goat's milk in the palm of her hand. Malinche Santistevan-Matthews was made of choices that were not her own. She was trapped by the rock walls men had placed around her. Malinche Santistevan-Matthews wanted to tear down that life. Stone upon stone she wanted to be free, maybe walk off into the trees and never return.

Mark Well How the Lilies Grow

Dear Ramon,

I am going to send this letter with your tio Nomio, so if you are reading it you know that I wished him my best and asked him to wish you the same. I do hope you are doing well. I miss seeing you in class and out in the fields. How are the mountains treating you? Your tio says that you are doing well, learning a lot, even reading some. His saddle-bags were full of letters and books. I suppose he is like a messenger to and for all the herders so I have no doubt this letter will reach you.

School is very different here. The nuns are nice, but they call me Nancy. One of them told me I would never get ahead in life with a name like Nonnatusia. Her name is Sister Cecilia. I do not like her, but there is a chance that she does not even like herself, she weighs close to a thousand pounds and never smiles. "Dear Lord forgive me for talking poorly about one of your servants but also grant her a little happiness." That is the prayer I say for Sister Cecilia. I think her last name is Ullrich. I'm sure I heard the priest call her that after church one morning. She teaches English and history. She has renamed everyone, I'm Nancy and Pedro is Pete, Jaime is James, Perla is Pearl, but she doesn't quite know what to call Dickey. It hurts her to say his name and she doesn't know what to shorten it to. Sometimes she calls him Richard but he never answers her. She'll say his new name about twenty times and he just won't look up from his book. I don't think Dickey will last long here. He gets in trouble every day and not just for not answering to his new name. If sister Cecilia were not as big as Mana Rufinita's cow, she might go up to Dickey's desk and hit him across the head, but instead she makes him go up in front of the class and swats him there. He is quite the character. This fall he got in trouble for answering Geronimo to one of Sister's questions. He answers everything Geronimo. His brother told him that was always a safe answer when he didn't know the real answer. So this fall the Sister asked us who discovered America. I don't know why she picked on Dickey, even called him by his real name. He answered that God and Geronimo discovered America. She made him come up to the front of the room for his paddling. She only hit him once because when she swatted him a huge cloud of dust came up from his nalgas. Sister was furious. She sent him to the office, but he told Sister Leander that he got swatted so much that his nalgas were all red. He told Sister Leander that his mom told him to put powder on his nalgas so that they wouldn't get blisters. You should have seen the cloud and Sister Cecilia's face. Dickey didn't get in trouble and now sister doesn't swat him on the nalgas anymore. She only hits him on the hands.

Sister Cecilia is always saying how us kids from the country get her goat. We don't really know what that means, but we know she has a lot of goats and that she doesn't like us. Dickey calls her Sister Many Goats, because we keep getting her goat and every time we do there is always another one.

Esperanza, the girl that used to sing on the rock in Santa Rita, is still going to school here. She can't read and the nuns have her in a different group. They put us in groups by using bird names. The kids that can't read are Crows, because Sister Bernice said all they can do is squawk. I'm a Cardinal because I can read well. I've never seen a real cardinal, but the pictures of them sure are pretty. If you were here we would both be Cardinals, I'm sure of it.

I really enjoy reading your letters. I've saved both of them and I am looking forward to hearing from you again. I'm sorry I haven't written to you sooner. I just didn't know what to say. I liked that poem too. I asked Sister Cecilia if we could read it in class but she says that we don't read Germans in America. She said that all the Germans are evil and are going to hell. She told Dickey he was going to hell too. He didn't seem to care. I care.

What books is your tio taking for you to read? We read some poems by this man named William Blake. I really liked them. There is one about a lamb and another about a tyger, that's the way he spelled it. I'm not sure but I think he is saying that God makes good and bad, lambs and tigers. I don't know if that means there is no devil or if God made the devil or what, but I know it explains why Sister Cecilia is so mean. I really like the poem about the lamb, of course I thought of you and it felt nice. It feels like when you are cold and someone brings you a blanket. I hope you are staying warm.

Your tio said that you are making me a present. He wouldn't tell me what it is, but he said it was very rare and that people pay a lot of money for this very thing in other countries. I asked him if you had found gold, but he only smiled and said this thing is just as rare but was living once.

I guess that rules out gold. Not that I want gold, I was just guessing so that your tio would give me a hint. Honestly, you could not bring me a thing and I would be completely happy with just a letter from you.

How does your tio know about other countries? I thought the nuns had seen the world, at least that is what they tell us. One of them said she has been to Kansas, but that is not another country. Your tio is a nice man. He has a good smile. Now I know where you get your smile from. Maybe one day you and I can see the ocean together. I think the Pacific is the one I want to see. I imagine it sometimes, the waves and their sound, the sand all dark and soaked through, I imagine you there too. I guess that means I care for you.

If any of the Sisters knew I was writing to you they would probably paddle me good. I'm supposed to be working on a paper about how Columbus discovered America. The more I read about it though, the more I think Dickey was right by saying Geronimo. Did you know that all of those discoverers, well most of them anyway, were just lost. That doesn't seem like discovery to me. I like to know where I'm going and where I've been. That way I can appreciate it when I finally arrive. I miss Santa Rita, almost as much as I miss you, but then again you are Santa Rita and so am I, all us kids and our parents, you know what I mean. I wonder who discovered Santa Rita and if they were lost. I think it is too perfect a spot for someone to find while they were lost. Whoever it was knew where they were going. I'm sure of that. This place is not that way. It is nice and everything, but it is here because of the train. Santa Rita is there because someone must have loved it there. That is the best sort of discovery I would say, one that leads you to love something, somewhere or someone.

Take care Ramon. I miss you. Thank you for the gift, in advance. I'm sure I will love it. May God Bless You and look over you.

Love,

Nonnatusia

Causes For Stumbling Should Come

Luke 17:1

The nuns called her Hope. She couldn't read, but she wrote
songs in blue ink. The songs were in a red tablet and no one
saw them. She dreamt the way all of us do, in broad and
bright colors. She saw herself on a stage, any stage really,
and the music would be in the room, living like a person
would live if everything were perfect, that's how the music
would be. The people would rise from their tables at the first
recognizable note. Some of them would go hand in hand
onto the wood dance floor. The dancers would move to the
music that lived in the room and then her voice would come
in, soft and in time with the music. The song was usually a
slow one, that's how she dreamt it and then wrote it in her
red tablet. Her voice was the living part of the song, the part
that could waver from the notes. Her voice was the part of
the song that could weep and sound exactly like crying. The
saxaphone would try and cry too, the trumpet would fill
the room with its version of pain, the guitar would come
in sad like something lost, but only her voice would make
the people dance closer, slower, only her voice would bring
what people were feeling together with how they were mov-

ing. Her voice was what saved people, and that is how she dreamt it, there in the Palace Hotel, room eight.

Her mother had named her with a prayer really. Her mother had named her to go beyond what she had done. It was the nuns that took three syllables and two vowels from her name, but that didn't change her mother's prayer. She knew the nuns meant well. She knew that Americans were afraid of too many vowels, everything had to be easy and too many vowels got in the way, slowed things down. Her mother had come with the train and its men. Though she never knew him, one of them was Hope's father and it was his voice that made its way into the little girl. It was his voice, his only gift to both of them before he left. Hope was not really from Santa Rita, but when her father left and there was no one, the mother did what she had to. She found a man who said he would look after both of them. This man left too, but at least he left them with a crumbling adobe. The house had two floors but no one dared go up to the second, for fear that they might fall through the rotting floors. Hope and her mother stayed there in the falling house and the girl's mother sent her to school. School is always the first part of a dream and Hope did not have to walk far to begin her mother's dream. The mother never expected her daughter to sing. She wanted her to go to school and learn something that would hold her for a lifetime. She didn't want her daughter to roam like she had. This place, this valley, this canyon of river cut stone, this is the last place she would ever go. That is what the mother told herself, but then Hope could not read. This too came from her unknown father. This second inheritance, this mark in the blood, would seek to cancel out the only gift he left her. The father had never loved the mother or Hope. It was an accident. That is what he said. Like falling off a horse, he said. Do I have to buy the horse because I fell off it, is what he said. That is the way with accidents, they break things for years. Accidents break things in increments and there was no way of knowing how deep the brokenness went and which part would need fixing first. Hope could not read, the letters were like seasons that fell out of order. So her mother did the only thing she knew. She moved her daughter into town so the nuns could teach her how to read.

All the girls from Santa Rita stayed at the Palace Hotel. Hope stayed in room eight which opened up to the lobby with its crushed velvet sofas. The other girls were nice to her, but she did not want to study with them. She stayed in her room and wrote songs in blue ink, songs with words as stilted and falling as her old house in Santa Rita. Only she knew what the words meant. She had asked the nuns if she could join choir but they told her that she would not be able to read the songs. She didn't need to read them, she understood the music, felt it, knew where the beats should step, where the melody was going. She knew all this instinctively and heard it as she wrote her own songs. She wanted to be in choir. She wanted her voice to come out and then people would love her. At times she would sing to herself, or jump up on a rock and sing to whoever would listen. All the kids knew she could sing, but the nuns did not even listen to her talk.

Hope did not intend to listen in on the conversation of Thomas B. Catlin. It wasn't even that she was interested, but she could hear him talking about the planes. If anything it was the planes that caught her interest. Hope wanted to know about the planes, who would come in on them, what it was like to fly. She wanted to write a song about flying, so she listened.

All the other girls were in the restaurant studying. They had invited Hope but she did not want to go. She was embarrassed that she couldn't read. Mr. DeLeon owned the hotel and he assured Thomas Barnes-Catlin that all the girls were in back studying . The two men talked a long time but Hope did not understand. Then she recognized a name, Ubaldo Hernandez, one of the herders from Santa Rita.

"How did you do it?"

"A rifle. Shot him right off his horse."

"Dead?"

"Checked him myself. Eyes were already going hazy by the time I reached him."

"Did he know?"

"Had one of the packages in his tent. Opened it too."

"Any of it missing?"

"No, dumb son of a bitch probably didn't know he could've been rich."

"Then why?"

"Who knows who that damn fool told. Better off cutting out the tongue and the whole mouth with it. Hate for him to go and weave some wool blanket telling the whole world about some box he found out on the llano."

"There's no one out there though."

"Ramon Fernandez is out there. Not far from that Ubaldo either."

"You think he knows?"

"That's why I'm here. You said he writes to that girl upstairs. You deliver the mail right?"

"Yes."

"Next letter that comes in gets lost. You hear me?"

"What are we going to do about Ubaldo?"

"Crows and the coyotes will take care of things."

"But his sheep, they'll roam. Someone will notice."

"Let 'em. There won't be nothing left of Ubaldo by morning. I'll make sure of that. Coyotes will have themselves a good time with his sheep too. By the time they round up the whole bunch and find what's left of him they'll think he died of a heart attack or something. Fell right off his horse, like an accident caused by natural causes."

Hope listened and wrote. The letters were all wrong, but she knew what the words meant. She pressed so hard on her red tablet that the broken words could be read two sheets below the one she was actually writing on. The two men discussed the planes and Mr. DeLeon agreed to pick up the boxes, seven of them, and bring them back to the hotel for Thomas Barnes-Catlin. Hope heard Catlin's heavy steps as he left the lobby. She waited for a second set of boots to move across the floor. She was afraid to move. They had killed Ubaldo for what he might have known. She knew more than Ubaldo and did not move at all. Finally, DeLeon rose and walked slowly across the floor. Hope heard the ringing of the cash register and the knocking of the cash drawer as it opened. She could hear Mr. DeLeon counting out loud to himself. He counted twice and then the drawer rang shut.

Hope prayed there in her room, still afraid to move. She prayed that the girls would not come in from the kitchen and knock on her door. She prayed they wouldn't come to her door and call out her name. She prayed they wouldn't bring her the homework. Most of all she prayed that Mr. DeLeon would go home, just walk out the door like he did every evening, lock up things behind him, check the door twice and go home. She prayed he would go home, just leave before the other girls came to her door and told the whole world that they all weren't in the back studying.

She did not know whom to tell. Nonnatusia had always

been nice to her, not made fun of her for singing on the rock. She could tell Nonnatusia, but she would tell Ramon and then too many people would know. If Ramon knew they would kill him too. She liked Ramon but she did not know whom to tell. If she were Apollonio, she would sing it in a song for everyone to hear, a sad corrido about the murder of Ubaldo. Apollonio was not afraid of anyone, she remembered that, her mother had told her about a man who came with the railroad, a giant of a man who one day would not stop drinking and refused to leave the cantina. The man had beaten his way through everyone who came near him, like a train breaking through the mountain snow her mother said. Her mother said how everyone was afraid except Apollonio. She would tell Apollonio, he would know what to do. She would leave after school. She would walk the back way home so that no one would see her. She would walk across the llano and over the mesa and drop into Santa Rita from above. She would not take the road. She would be quiet; no one would notice her walking the fifteen miles to Santa Rita. She would hand the blue letters and the broken words to Apollonio and then she would do like her mother taught her. She would run, maybe go to Santa Fe or El Paso. She would go to a place where she could sing in Spanish, somewhere with a stage and a band. She was afraid of Thomas Barnes-Catlin, she was afraid of the nuns, she was even afraid of words in books, but after tomorrow she would walk away from Santa Rita, Apollonio would tell her where to go. He would tell her where to go and not be afraid. Nothing would stop her. She would not stumble.

That night she packed a small bag of clothes and her only other pair of shoes. She would leave them in the alley and pick them up after school. She would keep the tablet with her. She would keep the songs close to her and when she got to the cantina she would rip out the last page she had written on and hand it to Apollonio. He would sing the words in a song and maybe the men would go for Ubaldo's body. She wouldn't wait to hear Apollonio sing the song. She would be far away by then, but she would imagine his voice, his crooked guitar and she would finally be heard.

Into the Lonely Places

Luke 8:29

He had seen their frozen bodies, and that is what stayed with him. He tried often to forget their hands. It was their hands that haunted him, the way they died last, always clutching and then stiffening in the positions he remembered and could not shake. Aresando was not afraid of dying. He was reckless and some said crazy, but this was his way of not being afraid of death. It wasn't that he loved Malinche San-tistevan-Matthews and could not live without her. He had done that his entire life. His parents loved him, and he knew that his mother prayed for him in the early mornings. It's not that he wanted to die either. Aresando was in that place between living and dying and that is why the hands haunted him. What last thing were they reaching for? What could there be worth grabbing at on the frozen ground around that damn reservoir? Santa Rita was more beautiful, people even respected him in the way they respect things they fear. He was in between, and every dangerous thing he did would lead him away from the middle. He just wanted a place.

Aresando watched as the man entered the Rio Lounge. He wore white and had to duck to get through the door.

There was a noise that followed the man as he walked toward the bar. Aresando had heard it before, the sound of a wagon on gravel, the crunching of wheels, the low rubbing sound of friction where the axle met the hub, a sound that if left unattended would lead to rust. He was sure he was the only one that heard the sound, and it did not stop, even when the man did. He could hear the wagon being dragged slowly across the dirt and gravel, recognized that the sound only came with a heavy load. He knew the sound and was sure that he alone heard it. The man in the white suit danced well, he noticed the man's left hand, every finger had gold. He watched the man's hand as it glided up and down Malinche's back. His right hand never left her hip as they danced. He heard the wagon, slow and consistent, watched as the man's gold hand fluttered between Malinche's shoulders and the small of her back. The song was slow and he hated Apollonio for playing it. He looked over toward the stage and saw that both of the guitar players were watching the man. He saw it in Apollonio's eyes, recognized the stare. Apollonio heard it too, the wagon groaning over a dirt road. Apollonio had been to all the wars, of course he would know the sound; it comes differently to every group of people, but in Santa Rita it was a wagon that they heard. Most do not recognize it, but Aresando did. He had heard it there in the cold near the reservoir. Apollonio heard it too. The two men met with their eyes and the guitar player nodded at Aresando.

Nomio was watching the man, too. He watched him the way a person watches a snake, but without fear. He seemed to be memorizing the way the man in the white suit moved. Nomio's hands moved effortlessly over his guitara de los dos cuernos. Nomio followed the man and the light that was around him. He did not hear the wagon the way Apollonio did, but recognized the way the man moved. The man moved like a leaf on water, a small boat across a wide river, he moved like a small boat across a wide calm river.

Aresando tried to meet Nomio's eyes, but the great herder with the shiny shoes and enormous hat would not look away. Aresando could hear the song ending, he knew it by the sound of Rafael's piano, the way it began its progression toward softness and then silence. Aresando thought of taking Malinche by the hand, pulling her from the dance floor and running into the darkness. She would not go with him, he knew this already. He did love her though. He loved Malinche, loved her the way people love what they cannot have, from a distance and with awe. He loved her the way people love the stars or the top of a mountain. In his heart he loved her like thunder, loudly consuming the earth with its sound, his love was thunder, it grew one loud explosion after another, loved her like thunder loud and untraceable, loved her in a way that could not be denied.

Outside he found the stars, looked for the queen, upside down in the sky. That was north, more north to him than the star at the end of the dipper. He had set his course to a queen who knew her own beauty and was punished for it. He watched the sky; there was no moon and he dreamt of leaving. He would follow the stars of the queen and forget this place forever. He loved his mother and father. None of this was their fault. He had been born with it. He had never cried and therefore was never truly happy. As he thought this he realized that he had come close a few times, catching Edimundo's perfect game, helping Malinche push her deer from the schoolhouse. They had touched hands that day. He pretended it was an accident, even apologized, but he had meant all along to put his right hand on her left, he had meant to feel the soft skin of her wrist and the delicate hair of her arm. It was childish, something a stupid kid would do, but he had done it anyway and could not forget it. That is the way with those types of memory, entire years can be lost in a moment, years can disappear and be replaced by memories of the slightest touch. Her hand was warm, smooth as milk in a bucket, soft like that, rich like that, warm, he loved her then and still did. He turned back toward El Rio Lounge and he walked toward the sound of Rafael's piano, the two guitars, and the sound of gravel beneath wooden wheels.

Most of the bueyeros left after that night. Not far, just to another valley. Enos' field, where they had first arrived, was left fenced and the river followed its course toward their new home. There, they were able to live alone and buy the water as it passed. It was a bueyero that saw the man's feet.

Aresando waited as the man in the white suit circled toward him. The night was very cold. The breath of the people mingled and before it rose the man moved in and out of the cloud. He seemed made of it, the breath of humans. He came at Aresando slowly, his right arm was behind him and his left was held up, hand in a gold fist just below his chin. Aresando did not move. Rafael was still playing the piano and that was the only sound. He was close to Aresando now, close enough to throw his punch, but he waited. Aresando stood, left foot forward, both hands up, and he waited too. He told himself that he would take the first punch, the left and then duck the right and come up under the man's arm, throw him to the ground and fight him where everything was even. He could not let the man fall on top of him. He would have to be on top if he was going to have a chance. The big man faked with his left, Aresando expected it and did not move. He had tackled the man inside, he fell like any other man and that was what he would do this time.

It was the right hand, the one he wasn't expecting. It caught him beneath his left eye and Aresando felt the blood immediately but did not wait for a second punch. He rushed the man, wrapped his arms around him and tried to push him off balance. The devil's knee came up as Aresando tried to tackle him. The knee came up hard into Aresando's nose and Aresando fell back, trying to break his fall with both hands. The devil was on him now, he could smell his breath, feel the ring of his right hand cut into his skin. He tasted the blood, felt the frozen earth at the back of his head, his hands pinned beneath the larger man's knees. He heard the wagon clearly now, the gravel popping beneath its wheels. His left eye was full of blood, he could barely see, but he heard Malinche's voice yelling for the two to stop. Her voice was full of tears. Aresando brought his right knee up, hard and into the kidney of the larger man, the wagon wheels grew more faint. He could hear the piano now. The devil, only for a second, lost his rhythm as one of his punches missed. Again, Aresando brought his knee up and this time the larger man was off balance. With his right arm, Aresando pushed against the man's leg, it moved and his arm was free. The blood was going down the back of his throat, he felt it cutting off his air. The devil reached for Aresando's neck. Aresando, with his free hand, punched the devil in the neck. He did it again, the second time with an open hand, driving his fingers into the devil's neck where it met his thick chest. He did it a third time and finally the man fell back clutching at his neck, coughing for air. Aresando stood and spit the blood from his mouth. His left eye had closed shut. He heard Malinche crying. Someone yelled out "now." Aresando blitzed the devil as he tried to stand. The top of Aresando's head met the other man's face and there was the sound of bone breaking. The blood from the devil turned black in the cold air. Aresando had fallen over him and was trying to stand when the bueyero screamed. As the devil had fallen backward his shoe was left in the dirt. The devil stood and faced Aresando, both of them full of blood. The bueyero was screaming. He shouted scripture from memory. The moon was rising late, Rafael's piano sounded into the night, the moon came through the cottonwoods, the bueyero prayed and pointed and then someone else screamed. The moon was waxing through the cottonwoods and its light caught the devil's feet. Someone else screamed and began to pray. The devil smiled through the blood and moved toward Aresando, his hoof clicking against the frozen ground. Aresando waited and tried to breathe through the blood in his throat. Mana Virginia broke the circle and walked toward both of them. Apollonio and Nomio came between the two and devil smiled at Apollonio, as though he recognized him. He moved toward the two guitar players, neither moved. The devil pointed at them and smiled again. He wanted to end it there. The moon broke over the trees and Mana Virginia walked toward the devil. The bueyero prayed and the devil turned to face the old woman. Aresando noticed that the wagon was no longer making its sound. All of them turned toward Mana Virginia. The devil took a step toward her and Nomio went to cut him off but it was too late. From her apron she had pulled two small bottles and removed the corks. The devil took a second step and she did not falter, she flung the contents of the two bottles at the devil and he began to scream. She did it again and again until both bottles were empty. She pulled two more from her apron, but there was no need. The devil ran toward the place where the circle had been broken. Aresando fell to the ground and Elle and Samuel ran toward him. Apollonio and Mana Virginia followed after the devil until they reached the trees. He was running toward the mesa and they could hear his screams. Both of them stopped and Apollonio smiled at her. She did not smile back at him, but she acknowledged that the devil would not return that night.

Later that year, Malinche would leave Santa Rita for Denver. She told her father and mother, but no one else. She boarded the train during the night. She walked through the steam of the idling train and took a seat near the window. She waved to her parents and almost cried. Her father smiled at her and seemed happy. Her mother only waved, and as the train began to move, blew her only daughter a small kiss from a gloved hand.

Aresando never stood in the saddle of his motorcycle again. His left eye had scarred nicely but he could not see out of it clearly. He told everyone his balance was off. After the fight he would sleep late into the evening and had finally found his place between living and dying. He moved into the lonely places of himself, driven by the demon. He was still called crazy and brave. No one blamed him for what he had done that night. He healed in time, his skin mending itself and only leaving marks where the cuts were deep. He would sleep until evening and then leave his parents house in the dark. He would go to the cantina and order two whiskeys and a water. He could not sleep at night. The frozen hands were always in his dreams, the sound of the wagon grinding across the road was constant now. He would enter the cantina and order two whiskeys and a water. He wondered if he could find himself now. He walked outside and, with his good eye, found the upside down queen. From under the eaves of the cantina there were newborn sparrows crying in their mud nests. There were five nests and he thought of smashing them. He looked toward the north stars and thought of Malinche, her soft hand. He walked back into the cantina and ordered another water and two whiskeys. He finished them and walked over to Apollonio who had just finished playing his crooked guitar. Apollonio had been in many wars. He was the best shot in Santa Rita.

"Do you think I'm crazy?"

Let Us Erect Three Tents

Luke 9:33

The light from the farolito filled the tent with orange. Nomio sat across from his nephew as he filled another cup of coffee. Outside the night was cold and both herds mingled in the rodeo. To the west and north of them the coyotes were yelping and crying into the November night. Ubaldo's horse and the two others, la palomina and Ramon's bay, were looking toward the sound of the coyotes, measuring it with their upright ears and flared nostrils. Ubaldo had raised his horse with a bottle after its mother died. Ubaldo had told Ramon how his horse was the best friend he ever had, smartest friend too, and then he would smile. Ubaldo believed that if he were ever to come back to life he would like to come back as a horse. Everyone joked with him and told him that he would finally have to start working if that were the case. He would joke back, telling them that at least he would gain some smarts if he were a horse. All the herders would laugh and someone would tell the story of Ubaldo's horse. They had all heard it so often that any of the seven could deliver it from memory.

Nomio drank his coffee slowly and motioned toward the horses and their rustling.

"That yegua of Ubaldo's is still smelling those coyotes."

"She is a good horse, stayed with him, not even the crows touched him."

"His yegua loved him. He raised her, from a potranca. She never knew her mother."

Ramon knew the story, he had heard it up high, around the campfires of Blue Lake and los brazos. He knew how the mother yegua had been too old, how her insides ruptured when the potranca was born. She hadn't died right away, but Ubaldo could tell she was sick. There was blood in her milk and she couldn't stand. She had been a good horse too. He cried for her, patted her neck and remembered all the campaderos the mother yegua had led him to. She had a good spirit, never tiring, a good walker that always broke into a run when the path rose to a steep hill. Ubaldo patted the neck of the mother yegua and apologized to her. He took the pistol from his saddlebag and apologized to her again.

"He had other horses," Nomio continued, "but that yegua was good blood. So he raised that potranca with a botella and a teta."

"Goat's milk," Ramon interjected.

Mana Virginia had a red she-goat with a white blaze down the center of her head. The goat would follow her to the apple tree and never protested as Mana Virginia tied its cuernos to the tree. Some people claimed the goat was as old as she was, but Ramon never believed that. It wouldn't have mattered what goat Mana Virginia tied to the tree. The important thing was that she was the one that milked it. This was the important thing.

"He didn't even have to break that horse. He just talked to her a little and explained how things would work. I lost five dollars that day. I was sure she would throw him, but he just talked to her, told her how the saddle and the blanket would fall on her spotted back, told her the bit would taste like the bottom of the grain bucket, that the freno and its reins would rest on her head and neck. He just talked to her and got right on. Lost five dollars that day."

"How long did she stay with him, you know, after?"

"Looked like two days. She was thirsty. The body was swollen like after two days."

"Are you going to the funeral?"

"No, I'll stay with you. I took him back to his family, helped prepare him. I told them where I would be. They understood."

"Do you think it is the same ones that killed my papá?"

"I don't think so."

"Why do you say that?"

"Ambrose left everyone going crazy down there. No one knows exactly how much he sold, but there is no water and very few trees here. They only buy trees and water. Whoever killed Ubaldo...

Nomio hesitated and Ramon could see that his uncle knew who had done it.

"Who?"

"Apollonio would not tell me, but he went to town the day I came to deliver Ubaldo to his family."

Ramon thought of Nonnatusia, of the lights of town he looked toward when the nights were clear, and when the clouds remained after sunset he could see the glow of the town, white and orange, reflected in the haze. He had read her letter so many times that summer. He felt for it now, his hand moving instinctively toward his breast pocket. It was there, folded and soft, the paper had taken the shape of Ramon's chest, the oil from his fingers had turned the edges of the letter brown.

"In the morning you should go to her. I'll wait with the herd. Bring her back here. She'll be ready. Apollonio has spoken to her parents."

"What's wrong?"

"Take my horse. Let her ride it. Come back right away. No ice cream, intiendes?"

"But,"

"She'll be fine, Apollonio and I will take care of things."

"For Ubaldo?"

"For all of us."

Nomio opened the small stove and reached for the dry wood next to it. The stove lit up his face and the light fell on his chest. Ramon watched as his tio placed the wood carefully on the original heart of the fire. The dry wood lit immediately and more light wrapped itself around Nomio, his hand seemed gold as he brought it away from the fire and closed the door to the stove. Ramon looked up, and even with the stove closed the light had not left his uncle. For a moment Ramon felt very young, his body was very young just then, it floated above Ramon and he could see the river where his father had taught him to fish, he could see his own young body floating in the light from his tio's body, his abuelita was there and she sent him for salt, he ran through the light toward the house, the bag of salt weighed nothing in his hand, he ran with it back through the light and felt it on his skin, he felt the light from his abuelita's fire, the chich-arrones were dancing in the boiling manteca of the caldera, he handed her the salt and she hugged him, her hands were paper from a bible as she touched his face, he felt safe there in the light of his abuelita, he missed her, he remembered her there in that moment and looked toward his tio, made of the same light, and again he felt safe and young.

"Will there be three tents," Ramon asked.

"Three?'

"Ubaldo's, for his things, his saddle, his grain, the bags of salt. The sheep will get into them. We should bring his tent here to the cerrito. You and I will stay in the second, this tent, and we'll need a third for Nonnatusia."

"Tomorrow morning you should leave early. I'll get things ready to start home with the sheep after I load Ubaldo's things on his yegua and bring them back here."

"You won't have a horse."

"I can walk. I have beautiful boots."

"We'll leave when Nonnatusia and I get back?"

"The next morning. We'll be home by evening. You can lead Ubaldo's horse. Tu novia can ride yours." He smiled, and Ramon smiled back

"Will everything be alright?"

"No mijo, but we must go home anyway."

"Nonnatusia?"

"Tomorrow and the next day she will be fine. After that the two of you can take care of one another." Again he smiled at Ramon.

"What do you mean?"

"Tomorrow you give her that gift you worked on all summer. Apollonio knows the future, but even I can tell that after tomorrow all things will change. You'll be happy, Ramon. Tomorrow, after she hugs you, remember that feeling, the way it went clear through you and made you feel light. Hold that feeling Ramon, it will keep you."

"What feeling?"

"You should try and sleep. You won't be able to, but you should try. After tomorrow you won't ask crazy questions like 'what feeling.'"

Ubaldo's sheep had finally settled into the new herd and fallen quiet. Off in the north the coyotes howled in the dark and Ubaldo's horse sniffed the air and neighed into the night, maybe calling for her mother, both of them.

Let Him That Has Ears to Listen

Luke 8:8

The girl was not real, only imagined in a dream. She played a violin that her father had given her for Christmas. Ramon was not especially fond of the violin, but that is what he dreamt. In the dream the field belonged to Ramon, everything had not been stolen from his father. The water rose cold in the May ditches and he yelled out across the vega that the acequia was alive. In the dream the girl had enormous cheeks and her hair curled naturally. She played the violin for him and the water rose in the field, overflowing from the ditches and out into the vega, the water was clear, the vegita was gold and brown from winter, the water flowed into the field and everything became the color of Nonnatusia's eyes, the field turned wet and dark, thirsty. Ramon woke from the dream and was happy. He loved the way his love made that field grow. He loved that his dream was of spring. His dream told him that Nonnatusia loved him too. He was happy after he woke and told his tio about the dream.

Ramon's dreams were well known because of what he saw in them. He didn't have the sight like Mana Virginia or Apollonio, but his dreams were more like a barrel left out to collect rain. His dreams collected what was already out there and transformed it into image. The girl in the dream came to him the way the dream about the horse, his bis-abuelo, and tia did. His dreams were always short and filled with repetition. He climbed out of the canyon to los brazos, the horse was at the top of the hill, the horse was missing a leg, the horse's right leg was gone and there was bone and blood, and then he would climb again to the same horse. He told his tio the dreams, both men had the same gift. Both could see far away into what had already happened with-out ever knowing that the events had already taken place. Neither could explain their dreams, but both accepted them and would wait for the dream to confirm itself. Ramon's dreams had always been accurate. His horse dream came to him, always the same horse, always missing the same leg. He told his tio and the two men rode to los brazos where Juan Herrera ran his herd. The horse was not dead, its leg was not even missing, but the dream had been accurate.

During the night Juan had risen to bleating sheep. Some-thing was in the rodeo and had scared the sheep into the night. He knew it was a bear. The black sow had come every night for the last week. He had lost eight sheep already and knew the bear always retreated to the east, down the hill from the camp. Juan rose during the night and fired two shots into the air. He could hear the heavy running of the sow through the trees, heard the branches beneath the ani-mal's weight, he could see her shadow in the aspen as she ran into the canyon. His third shot had been toward the moving shadow in the aspen. He had aimed carefully and fired at the moving noise and dark shadow. The next morn-ing his horse would not come for its grain. He searched for her near the ojito where he had left her. Ramon's dreams were always the same. He dreamt what was already true.

The third shot from Juan Felipe Herrera's rifle had entered the horse above her right leg. Juan found her in the deep aspen where the bear had been running. Ramon had dreamt the horse that night and was sad to be right. The three herders led the horse to a place where the grass was thick and the sheep had not been. They gave her all the grain she wanted and let her drink from the cool ojito. They left Juan with his injured animal as Ramon rode back toward the herd and Nomio went toward town to get him another horse. As the two rode away they waited for the echo of the bala. Both men dreaded it, but when it came they did not look back. They rode away from the sound of the rifle and Ramon hated his dream.

The other dreams were the same, his bisabuelo under an apple tree. Outside there was a storm and the wind blew, but the tree was calm, the apples were ripe and his bisabuelo was happy. He knew when he woke that the man had died, knew that his bisabuelo who fished the river beautifully was safe from the storm.

His tia came to him the same way, not in a storm but over and over. It was only her face in a mirror, a mirror that you are not looking at but see yourself in, the mirror was in Ramon's periphery but the image was not his. Over and over he walked across the hallway, the mirror was to his right and his tia was in it. She smiled but there was no way Ramon could have known that she had died unexpectedly. The word came days later and he remembered the dream immediately and finally understood.

He told his tio about the dream, how the girl jumped up on a cottonwood stump and began to play the violin for him as the ditches rose into the field. There was no storm, the horses worked their tails in the meadow and everything was calm, the lirios were budding purple, the water was cold, there were no mirrors like in his other dream, only the water reflected but that was not out of place. This girl in the dream played the violin for him. He knew it was his daughter, even then. He knew that Nonnatusia loved him because their girl was beautiful. He told his tio the dream, how everything was in place, how there was no storm, no mirror, no climb to an injured animal. Ramon told Nomio his dream because he told him all of these dreams, he told him because he woke happy that morning.

Nomio was happy for Ramon. The dream was a good one, not out of place, not like his own dreams where the dead came to him and said goodbye before leaving. His dreams were like Ramon's, unsettled and repetitive so he was happy for the dream of the girl playing the violin in spring.

As he listened to Ramon he remembered how his abuelo had come to him and sat on the edge of his bed. "No lo hagas jito." That is what his abuelo told him that night, so Nomio did not do it. He listened to his abuelo Enos who had pushed him from the wagon and saved his life years before. His grandpa came to Nomio that night and looked the way Nomio remembered him. "No lo hagas jito," and he didn't.

Ramon's dream brought Nomio's with it as they talked there in the tent. They talked and neither listened completely to what the other was saying. Both were coming back, in their own way, to what they had collected in their dreams. Nomio recalled how his friend had come to him from across the ocean, the Pacific. Jose Garcia had traveled across the Pacific during the night. He had traveled from the island where he had died. He came to Nomio to say goodbye. Nomio did not like his dreams and Ramon did not like his, but both men accepted them. They accepted that Jose Garcia had died there on that island with many others like him. There were no Japanese soldiers in the dream, but Nomio knew what had happened. Jose Garcia was not sad, none of them were sad in the dreams, they only came to say goodbye and that is why the dream of the girl with the violin was different. There was no one at the edge of the bed, there were no bombs or dead jungle, there were no mirrors, the apples were not ripe with Ramon's bisabuelo perfectly calm in the lightning and rain.

Ramon was happy as he finished telling his tio about the dream. Ramon rose from the tent and walked out into the meadow and looked out at the sheep spreading themselves up the hillside on the other side of El Rito Azul. Ramon's coffee was steaming in his hand, the morning had already left its dew, the sheep glided through the grass, the echo of their moving came back across the green meadow and the sun was coming. He drank the sweetened coffee and turned back toward the tent. He smiled at his tio who was coming into the dewy morning and looking toward the sheep.

"That was a good dream Ramon. A girl playing a violin, the water rising, a good dream."

"Yes tio, she was beautiful, her mother's eyes, my cheeks, the water rising in my own field."

"What song was she playing?"

Ramon's smile left him. It was the song. He had forgotten about the song. Ramon looked at his tio, but his smile was gone. He looked at his tio and Nomio saw that the dream was like the others. He regretted asking Ramon the question, he could see that the song was what made Ramon upset. It was the song that made the dream like the others.

I Am Not Strong Enough to Dig

Luke 16:3

Santa Rita, too, would give herself away in small pieces, like the frozen earth to a shovel. Santa Rita would disappear slowly and only a few would understand its loss. Santa Rita would die, but there are pieces of her with its people. Only a few would know how the town was carried with them. Only a few would know how loss was meant to be left alone. Only a few would understand how the loss eventually equals the healing.

Nonnatusia watched as Ramon walked across the January field. The gold grass was short and the rocks in the field were visible from the window. She watched Ramon as he made his way south toward a cedar tree the two had chosen together. There he would dig the grave for the two that were named. She said their names to herself and felt them again, the weight of their once anticipated birth in the soft part of her stomach. Ramon walked slowly and passed Lara's abandoned house, the only piece of land that Ramon's father had not lost, the land inherited from Ramon's abuelo. There was no roof on the house and the adobe walls were slowly being beaten back to the earth. The house was alone and empty with no trees to shelter it like the other houses. The beaten and empty house was Nonnatusia and she understood its existence and its fading completely.

She had known, even before Ramon's dream. Her womb was not right; there was pain but she believed that if she loved what was growing inside her that love could make all things right. She prayed too, silently, in the slim November light of the canyon. Now the days were short and the mesa held the sun from all but the center of the valley. Lara's house stood at the edge of shadow and light, but the tree Ramon walked toward would not feel the sun again until May. The lilacs along the ditch and the fences would come then too, but she did not think of their sweet purple smell, she did not think of the ditches rising on either side of the grave, she only thought of their two names, how they were old names filled with vowels, names that were supposed to hold some old part of the soul in them. The names were supposed to be beautiful and heal. She felt the weight of her angels. The priest had told her that they would enter heaven and be baptized by their desire to be with God. The priest told her that they would enter heaven as adults and without sin, that in heaven her two unborn children would be happy. She loved them for their perfection, she loved them because she believed they would make her whole, and she loved them more now that the two had left her injured and falling. She was Lara's house and no one could see that about her.

The women in Santa Rita told her that others had lost like she had. They counted on their fingers the women and the children they had lost. The women meant no harm; they meant to strengthen Nonnatusia with evidence of loss and how it could be overcome, but she did not need their words, they were echoes too distant to make out. She only heard that she should forget and move on, that a woman's strength is inherited and would hold her when nothing else could. She heard the echoes of the other women, how their voices persisted in the December of her loss. At times the voices weighed on her and she longed to be empty and alone, she prayed to God, Mary and Jesus. She prayed for the two whose names she kept repeating under her breath, she prayed for Ramon working in the cold sombra of the cedar tree beneath the mesa, she prayed to be left alone and stand the way she knew how.

All things tragic come with regret and blame. Nonnatusia worked at her table with only the small light of a farolito to light her reading. The light bounced off the sheets of music and the words that came with the dark notes spilling across the page. She blamed herself, felt responsible for what her body could not keep. She heard the song in her head, kept its melody with the fingers of her right hand, barely fluttering on the wood table. She would rise from the table and leave the song there. She would not come back to it for months. She tried to disappear in the song but it would not let her, and for a while she resented it. In her youth music was the place she would fall into when the need for falling was evident. She told Ramon that the great musicians had a cut in their soul. That is what she said. The cut could not heal itself, only the music could ease its bleeding. That is how she felt afterward, there was this cut inside of her and the blood could not find its way out. She searched through the sheets of music she had saved, she wrote her own songs but none of them eased her. The music was meant to be heard, that is the nature of its gift. It heals through the ears and through the mind and is pulled by the folds of the heart into the center of a person and that is where they heal, deep in the center of themselves, but no one listened to her song.

This is all true; there are different versions of Nonnatusia's love and how it had failed her, but this is the one that comes up here like a river rising. She believed all of her loves would save her, but more importantly that those loves, would save the two she and Ramon had named. She summoned them all, her loves like disciples pulled away from their boats, and begged them to follow her and ease her children to life. Afterward, as Ramon was walking toward the tree, she summoned her loves again, the music that had buoyed her, her family that knew her, Ramon who held her and cried with her, but none of them answered. She was alone now and understood completely the way things fall in pieces.

There is no way to put an abandoned house together again. You can only leave it to its own end. All falling is not sad. Sometimes it is necessary. Healing is a well, a single well in an open field. Healing is a house without a roof, healing is three walls where four used to stand. You cannot make the well water clean by filling the hole and you cannot raise a wall by looking at those that are still standing. There was no fixing Nonnatusia, she didn't need fixing, only a slow healing that would ease her as it smoothed her.

Ramon waved to her from across the field. He could see her in the window, how she never left it, how she looked south and did not wave back. The frozen earth gave itself up slowly and in small pieces. The grave was made of shadow and sat between two ditches. He waved again and this time her hand came up. He loved her and let her be silent. There was no other way. He went back to his digging, lowering himself to his knees and scooping the cold dirt with his hands. He had chosen this spot because it was a place where the echoes of children playing could be heard. He had chosen the spot because he had never known Lara, he only knew her abandoned house and rock lined well.

He had dropped stones into the well when he was young. He would wait at the lip of the dark hole for the water to answer him. He knew his wife was injured, he thought of el Profeta Isaias, and how the word of Jesus had come "para sanar los corazones heridos." He had heard about this healing in church, just after the two that were named had been baptized by their desire. The two names were written in the book of the dead and the priest would recite their names on el dia de los muertos. Hearing their names would ease Ramon, their names were written and that meant they existed.

The motion of his digging was settling in his muscles. He felt tired and only sought to finish and return to his wife. She was the only one who understood him and he knew that if they could be alone together both of them would be healed like the prophet had promised. They only needed to hear one voice and not the many. He loved Nonnatusia completely and sought to ease her by being strong. He had picked a spot to bury the two, a spot where he remembered being happy. He did not know that his wife, who waited at the window for him while he finished his work, had known this spot too. She knew if from a place that was deeper than any man can know. She knew the falling house and the boarded up well in a part of her that was consistent and real.

Everyone sought to heal them with their words. They sought to heal them by pointing out other children, how hope could still be born into the world. Ramon listened and sometimes even believed the voices, but as he scooped the grave clean with his bare hands and looked toward his wife, he knew they would have to heal alone. Maybe the word of Jesus would bring them solace, but otherwise they were alone, and only the abandoned house knew their loss.

If These Remained Silent the Stones Would Cry Out

Luke 19:40

The cold did not bother Aresando; that first October snow of 1958 did not enter him. He had felt the cold once when he was eighteen, felt what real cold was. Back then he only wanted to come home for Christmas, to sit next to a fire his father had built. He wanted only to sit in the kitchen and laugh in the warmth.

Some of the other men told him that the wind that December was more than a hundred degrees below zero. In Santa Rita he had never known real cold; he thought he had, but nothing was like that reservoir. Men froze during the night and never woke, but really no one slept, it was the cold that entered them until some of them even began taking off their jackets, some of the men said they were warm and began to unbutton their clothes. That seemed the strangest way to die, in the cold complaining of being warm. Aresando had learned to recognize it then, the way the brain will lie to you in order to save you from pain. He had heard that drowning people, after they accept the water, take a final breath and then it is as though they are sleeping.

That is how the men died in the cold, sleeping.

He wasn't sure about drowning, but he decided that when he wanted to die it would be in the cold. He would ride his motorcycle out into the llano and find himself a solitary tree. He would wait for a time, admire the stars, maybe count them and name their formations. Afterward he would lie down at the base of the tree. He wouldn't take a jacket. A jacket would only tempt him and probably save him. He would ride out into the llano and lie down next to a cedar or juniper tree and shiver there in the cold. He would shiver until his body told him he was getting warm, until his brain began to lie to him. He would ride so far out on the llano that he wouldn't be able to change his mind. He would lie down beside a tree and wait for sleep. He had the plan in his head. He knew his mother would believe it was an accident. She would think her only son had gotten drunk and stopped to rest and never made it back up. This plan would save him and his mother. He practiced it in his head, how he would walk into the cantina and order more whiskeys and water than ever before. He would walk out into the dark and start his motorcycle. He would rev the engine so that everyone would hear. He would rev the engine until someone came out and told him it was too cold to be riding. Then he would turn the bike south and move with his lights off over the rolling hills toward the big volcano. He would avoid the camps of the herders and move east, out into the open llano where no one ever went. He would ride with his lights off and find a good tree by smelling it in the cold air. His plan was flawless. He would wait beneath the tree and listen to the wagon roll over the frozen road. He would listen to it roll toward him and when it went silent he would join the others, the others that made up the wagon's heavy load.

Malinche Santistevan-Matthews had a similar plan, not for her death, but like Aresando, for her freedom. She thought of it often, the way she had watched Mana Virginia put the cow down.

Everyone had heard about Mana Rufinita's cows, her two red cows, both virgins, both old and held together by their hides stretched thin and tight over protruding bones. Mana Rufinita had had the cows since they were terneras; she had traded a rifle and a saddle for them. The rifle had been her husband's and the saddle belonged to her father. Both men had died, her husband in the first war, her father had died of the things that fathers die of, his age and his work. She had saved the rifle, a lever action .30-.30 with flowers and swirls engraved in the metal. It was a heavy rifle with dark wood and gold metal. She had saved it because it was her husband's and that was one way of remembering him. The saddle was a fine piece of craftsmanship, over a hundred years old, with a horn thicker than a man's forearm and wider than his palm. The black leather had silver buckles and its tassels were cut long and thin. She had saved them both for years and never used them. The two cows were only a year old when she traded for them. She was reluctant at first to part with the rifle and saddle, both were part of her, but the other women had told her that she could get milk from the cows, that she could sell the calves or trade them for a rifle and saddle every year. The other women told her that by the time the cows died she would have so much milk and so many calves she could trade for all the saddles in Santa Rita, and so she parted with a bit of her past and immediately loved the two cows more than she expected. She loved them so much she could not imagine them with a smelly bull mounting them, she could not imagine her two red cows having to bear the weight of an obtuse animal like a bull. She protected their virginity and neither cow gave milk or had a calf, and that was fine with Mana Rufinita. She protected her cows for sixteen years until Edimundo Trujillo's bull got loose and ran all over creation hopping fences. The bull was a worthless runt of an animal, not more than seven hundred pounds and with only one horn. The bull had been fenced in with six other cows, but he grew tired of them and jumped the fence. He jumped every fence in Santa Rita until he was out of fences. Mana Rufinita had chased off the speckled bull several times, chasing it away with a stick and prayers to San Francisco, the patron saint of animals and virgin cows. Edimundo Trujillo would come for his bull every morning, removing it from one field or another and by the afternoon it had jumped another fence and was on top of some cow. The other men were angry and threatened to kill the bull, such a runt could not breed their cows; all the calves would come out speckled and with only one horn. Edimundo tried to save the life of his bull, but the animal was as stupid as it was persistent. Finally, it jumped Mana Rufinita's fence one Sunday while she was in church. When the people came out of the church they could see that the bull had mounted one of the ancient cows. The other had refused him by falling to the ground under his weight. She was so old she could not support him and then afterward could not get back up. The one horned bull had mounted the virgin cow and that was how the bull was killed, shot in the head by Edimundo himself, a total embarrassment to the pitcher of the Santa Rita baseball team. The ancient cow was still loved by Mana Rufinita and she waited for the calf to be born. She did her best to feed the cow more hay, but the animal never got fatter, never dropped any milk into her ubre. The calf came in December 1956 and by some miracle of San Francisco was huge. The cow could not deliver it. She fell to the ground and strained her old bones against the emerging calf. Mana Rufinita could not deliver it either. She called to Salustiano and Juan de Jesus Sanchez to help her. The two men tied a rope to the front legs of the huge calf and tied the other end to Juan Sanchez' bay gelding. The horse strained against the taut rope and the cow was dragged behind the horse, the calf not budging. Both men, under Mana Rufinita's supervision, were allowed to reach into the cow and attempt to free the calf's head. It was Salustiano who noticed the calf had a horn, only one, that was holding the calf back. Mana Rufinita cursed the ugly bull and prayed to San Francisco. After three hours and two horses pulling, the calf was born, not with one horn but with two heads. It was alive and probably uglier than its father. The second head was without eyes and had no ears. It just protruded from the right side of the other head. Juan de Jesus Sanchez had gone for Mana Virginia and Salustiano had gone around telling everyone about the two-headed calf born from the formerly virgin cow.

That is how Malinche Santistevan-Matthews got the idea for her freedom, how she would escape her husband of less than a year. She was home visiting and not looking forward to going back to her old husband. She was making excuses about how she would leave later, much later, Karl wouldn't mind. Ponce, who was old and failing, would have nothing of her excuses. He insisted that a woman should be with her husband and he was about to force his daughter to leave when Salustiano came announcing the calf. Malinche could not believe her good fortune; even her father quit his complaining. Malinche, her mother, and her father left the house and walked with the curious crowd toward Mana Rufinita's field. Mana Virginia was already there. She told the crowd that the calf was supposed to be twins, but the egg had not divided. Everyone nodded and understood. The greater tragedy was that the cow could not stand up. She had been paralyzed by the birth. The cow's rear legs were useless, but she tried to rise and lick her calf clean. She strained against herself, rising on her front legs and then falling back to the ground. Someone offered to shoot the animal and put it out of its misery, but Mana Rufinita would not allow it. She gestured for Mana Virginia and the two women spoke in whispers.

Mana Virginia reached into her apron and pulled out a small leather pouch. Salustiano helped her raise the cow's head and some of the other men held the cow down. The animal did not struggle against them. Mana Virginia whispered something to the fallen mother and opened the pouch. She pulled out some ground leaves. Malinche Santistevan-Matthews recognized the plant. She had seen it growing on the mesa. She remembered watching as Mana Virginia searched among the rocks of the mesa for this very plant. The healer took the leaves and mixed them with a bit of water and looked again at Mana Rufinita who nodded her head. Salustiano opened the cow's mouth and Mana Virginia poured the mixture in. It didn't happen immediately, but very soon after the cow began bramando into the evening, the sound of her cry echoed for a bit and then she put her head down. She died peacefully.

Malinche Santistevan-Matthews smiled to herself, recalling the funny parts of the story, but then the smile left her as she came back to her plan, the dry leaves of the plant that Mana Virginia had used on the cow. She would wait until spring and go up to the mesa. She would gather the plant and mix it with mint from the riverbank. She would mix it with so much mint that a person could not taste the other plant. She would bring the mixture home and when her old husband came home she would welcome him with a cup of tea and then she would wait and finally be free.

Aresando rode south with his lights off. There was moon and stars to see by. He would turn off the paved road and head east. He kept his good eye focused on the left side of the road, searching for the gate and the dirt road that led to the open llano east of the highway. He would avoid the cerritos where there were camps. He would veer to the south and then go east again and park his motorcycle along an arroyo and fall asleep forever. He had the plan in his head when he heard the plane. It was flying low and toward him. He recognized the sound but he could not see the plane. It was flying with its lights off but it was close, flying above the highway. He pulled to the side of the road and listened as the engine grew louder in the cold air. His body was completely numb; already he couldn't feel his hands or feet. The muscles of his legs stung and twitched. Aresando looked back toward town and could see that there were lights on the paved road. He checked the moon and three stars of the hunter's belt. The hunter was already in the west. In a few hours there would be light, not enough time to freeze beneath a tree he told himself. The plane was over him now, he was sure of it. The lights on the highway were getting closer and he wondered who could be driving out so late. The thud almost startled him. There were three more thuds in the night, the last of them landed in the middle of the road, only a few feet from Aresando and his Indian motorcycle. Instinctively he knew what was in the box. It was small, the size of an adobe, wrapped in brown packing tape. He walked to the middle of the road and carried the package back to his motorcycle. Somewhere in the night he heard the plane's engine fade as it banked away from him and turned back to the south. The lights from the truck were close now. He straddled his idling motorcycle and drove south following the plane as it droned away. All together there were four packages and he stopped for all of them and one by one placed them in his saddlebags. He knew their contents and their destination. Varshant would go crazy. He was sure of it. He hated the viejo and hoped he would die of a heart attack when the drugs he was expecting did not arrive as planned. There would be nothing for the old bastard to deliver to Denver. Maybe someone up there would miss them so much they would kill Varshant for him. Aresando was growing tired of waiting for Malinche, he could wait for the viejo to die of a heart attack or be killed, but he wouldn't wait much longer to tell her how he loved her, how he had meant to kill himself in the cold but instead found the way he could finally be with her.

Mark Well How The Lilies Grow

Dear Ramon,

The gift you made for me is beautiful. I just wanted to write and tell you again how much I think of it and you.

These last few days have been crazy and I hope and pray that Esperanza is safe. I spoke with your tio as we drove the sheep home and he assures me that she is, but I just can't stop thinking about all that has happened. My father is very thankful to you and your tio Nomio for looking after me these past few days. I always thought a camp like that would be lonely, and it probably is the loneliest place in the world if you are all alone, but with you and your tio keeping me company and listening to his stories, it was one of the best things I have ever done.

I'm not afraid to say it now, even though it is probably not my place. I think I love you Ramon. There was something about the way you hugged me that day in town, the way your eyes looked when I unwrapped my gift. I can tell that you are a good person and I would like for us to spend all the time we can together. You know that bridge a few miles upriver from Mana Virginia's house, the one the sheep cross in spring on their way up the canyon. I would like for the bridge to be our place. If anything ever goes wrong and we need to see one another, I would like for that bridge to be the place. We can go there and you can keep one of your promises to me, teach me how to skip rocks.

Your tio is a great man and I am grateful to him for looking after the two of us. He kept you safe this summer and taught you many things. You seem so much bigger to me now, not that you've grown taller, you're just bigger and that is good to see. I can't explain it. I woke up the other morning in the tent and you had made a fire. You were just watching me sleep. You seemed happy just to be near me. That is how I felt too. To think of all the horrible things that have happened this summer, to Ubaldo, Esperanza running away, and a war going on across two oceans and here I am happy just to be in the same tent with you. It's funny how things like that work, when the world is its ugliest there is always a little piece of something nice to balance things. Do you think that if we were to put things on a scale and weigh them that the beautiful things, even though they are small and rare, would weigh as much as the ugly things, even though those things are big and always around?

I had never thought of anything like that until the other morning, the way the sun was rising and coming into the tent, your tio out with the herd giving them salt and you making a fire and watching me. I've spent the last few months in town and it is nice. There are things to do in town, people have cars and you can listen to music on the radio. There are three stores where you can buy food. There is another store where people can buy clothes and another one where you can get ice cream. We don't have to cook over there, we just go to the restaurant and they bring and take away your plate for you. It is nice there. Every morning I get to sing in choir and one of the nuns is teaching me how to play the flute. I guess what I'm saying is that town is a good place but I was never as happy there as I was waking up that morning out on the llano. What I'm really saying is that you might be able to put next to nothing in a scale, just a tent, the sun rising, a good fire, and some good company and it would weigh more than all the cars and ice cream in the world. Jesus was poor and he called himself a shepherd, and most of us would like to be like him but hardly any of us are.

I'm sorry that I'm going on and on, I'm getting to be like you. Just kidding, I love the way you are, the way your letters ramble and always say something more, something I was hoping to hear.

I am going to say goodbye for now. I am so glad that you are home and if this letter gets to you by Friday, I'll give it to your tio tomorrow so he can deliver it, then maybe you can teach me how to skip rocks. I'll wear my gift and you can see how it looks. You already know the place to go, so hopefully I will see you on Friday. I'll be there in the evening when all the birds start up again.

Please take care and thank you so much for all that you and your tio have done. I'll keep both of you in my prayers. I'll pray for good days and waking up happy. God Bless You Ramon.

Love,

Nonnatusia

It Is Toward Evening and the Day
Has Already Declined

Luke 24:29

The winter of 1956 brought an old dream to Nomio. The dream would wake him in the dim light of dawn; Nomio would rise from his wool mattress and look over Santa Rita, there was no light from kerosene lamps flickering in the windows, no smoke rising from the chimneys, even the corrals at the edge of the meadow were silent. Santa Rita was an old woman now, only her closest family members had stayed with her. Soon they would gather around her bed and they would pray into the night, ancient prayers that were like song, farewells.

Nomio had seen the ocean in the winter of 1944, smelled the salt of it, heard it come ashore. He had felt the water climb up his body and then break toward land. He had been to the Pacific at dusk to gather the spirit of his friend.

Jose Garcia came to Nomio in a dream. Nomio heard the dream. It was one word that woke him from his sleep. Leyte. Leyte. His friend repeated it until Nomio had fallen back into the dream and saw his friend where the water grabs at the earth and pulls it, in pieces, back toward the water.

Leyte, he had heard that in the dream. Jose Garcia repeated it to him and that is what Nomio remembered most about his dream. He knew then that he would have to gather what was left of his friend.

The body of Jose Garcia had arrived in November, 1944 and all the people had walked up the mesa behind the priest. There was a winter grave, the edges of it were the dull black of cinders from the fire the men had used to thaw the ground. They had broken through the frost three feet down and then had to contend with the rocks left by the river centuries upon centuries before. They began at daybreak when winter is coldest. The wind off the Sangre de Cristos met them up there on the mesa and entered them, but they dug against it; the fire they had lit the night before had burned itself to shades of white and blue ash. The men scooped the ash with their shovels and pushed it aside and began digging against the cold. The dirt from the grave mixed with ash, the sun rose and brought the coldest part of the day with it. They dug as the sun rose, its dim heat finally winning out over the cold it had spawned. They broke through the frost early in the afternoon. By evening they were done digging and removing the rocks; there was only the dark ring of the dead fire and a high mound of dirt. The next morning they buried the body of Jose Garcia.

Nomio rose the morning of the dream and packed only a small bottle Mana Virginia had given him. He had delivered Ubaldo to his family only months before. It had become his duty to collect the difunctos and bring them home.

Nomio saw the Pacific, felt its breath on his body, and it called to him. He removed his boots, his beautiful shiny boots, and walked in up to his waist. The water lifted him as it came ashore, weightless he fluttered his arms in the salty water and thought of his friend. The water lifted him again and pushed him toward the shore. He walked against the water and moved deeper into the ocean. The water at his feet ran back toward its mother as the waves at his chest pushed him toward their voice. It was their voice, the watery thunder of their voice that spoke to him, and it was the water at his feet rushing back out to sea that made him call out to his friend. Nomio's voice was lost in the waves meeting the sand. He could not feel the sand beneath him. The water carried him.

It had been twelve years since Nomio had traveled to the Pacific to collect what had not been buried on the mesa. Nomio remembered how he could not let the water keep his friend.

Too much had been lost or disappeared since that day. The old memory of the water carried him, weightless, as he thought of Ubaldo, Jose, the girl the nuns called Hope, Ramon's father, the land, the water, the herds, too much was still disappearing and again the ocean of a long ago dream had come to him, perhaps to ease the burning.

He had collected the body of Ubaldo, helped the herders move their animals off the llano when Ambrose Benedict-Matthews did not return, delivered the news of Ramon's father to his nephew, watched as the fences went up around Santa Rita, been powerless as the people's land had been purchased without their knowledge. He thought of the land.

Like the ocean that delivered Jose Garcia, Nomio was again made of water; he couldn't feel the earth beneath him and he knew what the people of Santa Rita were feeling. Weightless, he saw the rising mountains where they meet the meadows and the river. Before Ponce had sold, each of them had a piece of meadow and river, each of them had a piece of the mountain where it rose into the trees and high lakes. The water from the ocean was born up there. That very same dream water carried him now, and he knew his friend was with him. Jose Garcia was with him. Jose Garcia had died before coming home to find that his land, like Ramon's father's and all the others, had been sold or stolen.

Nomio recalled how his friend spoke of the land as though it were human. Jose Garcia called the land "she." The bueyeros called the land "it," but Jose Garcia and the people of Santa Rita referred to the land as family. The land was all that Jose Garcia had ever known. He loved her completely and followed her from the meadows to the high lakes. From the meadows she gave him food and from her belly she gave him wood to warm his home, and from her eyes she gave him water to drink and carry him home. Jose's only love had carried him across an ocean. Twelve years earlier, Jose Garcia's prayer was lifted in the winter snow and it came to Nomio in a one word dream. Leyte. Leyte. The dream fell on Nomio's sleep like the lightest of snows, the dream came in one word and was weightless as a single flake of snow. Nomio had answered the dream and waded into the Pacific. The water carried him now as it did then, and Nomio was the snow, he was his friend's way of returning to his home, his land, his love.

In the winter of 1944 Nomio dove until he came to the water that was running back into the ocean. He drank deeply, felt the salt burn at his throat and eyes. His body did not reject the water like he had expected. The ocean flowed into him, salty and cold. He rose to the surface and swam toward shore, the waves carrying him. His mouth tasted of salt, his feet met the sand and he began to walk ashore. He reached down and cupped the water in his right hand and let it fall into his left and then back into the ocean. He reached into his pocket and removed the bottle Mana Virginia had given him before he left. The bottle was full of water from Jose's well. Nomio drank half of it and the well water washed the salt from his mouth. Nomio fell to his knees right where the water began to move back into the ocean. He filled the bottle and replaced the cork. Nomio walked onto the sand and held the water up to the moon rising in the east. The air was cold, but it made him feel alive. The moon reflected in the glass and bent the water from the bottle back toward the voices coming ashore. Nomio placed the small bottle in his pocket and put on his shiny boots. He rose in the moonlight and began walking east, away from the ocean. He could still feel the water at his legs, the movement stayed with him and he was home by morning.

O Faithless and Twisted Generation

Luke 9:41

He looked different, between the wars, when Ambrose
Benedict-Matthews first met him. He was taller, heavier,
without hair and had a different name. His eyes were nar-
rower then too, they saw into people, and the one thing
that Thomas Barnes-Catlin could count on was the frailty
of people. There were seven sins, Catlin knew this, but he
also knew that he could not count on all seven to breathe
out of one person. What Catlin knew and what he used
was his knowledge that the appearance of one sin, let's say
greed, would bring about the six sins in the other people.
That is how Catlin worked; he seeped into the weak parts
of things, the frail parts of people and rotted everything
from the inside out. Ambrose Benedict-Matthews was an
easy mark. Greed was Catlin's bait.

It was passed to Ambrose Benedict-Matthews in a note.
The paper was folded once and had a watermark where the
sender had placed his drink. It was a simple note. It barely
registered with Ambrose Benedict-Matthews, because the
auctioneer's voice was like boiling water, repeating itself
and getting louder, hotter, the lambs were bringing a good

price that year, outside there were train whistles, and all around the sale barn people were talking and bidding on the lambs Ambrose had brought north. He folded the note the way it had been delivered to him. The little boy in the red shirt that had brought it over did not wait for a reply. The boy smiled at Ambrose Benedict-Matthews and gave the man a nod. It wasn't the type of nod a child would give, but Ambrose did not think of that then. He only noticed that the boy had no teeth. Then he turned back to the auctioneer barking "sold" into the semi-circle of people staggered upwards on the benches overlooking the sale ring. Ambrose Benedict-Matthews turned back to where the boy had been, but he was gone. He placed the note in his breast pocket and that is where it grew.

He sold nearly ten thousand lambs that day, his wallet thick with the money he owed to the herders. He sat down for dinner at the Oxford Hotel, ordered fish and a wine that suited his taste. He hadn't thought of the note or the little boy but as he waited for his meal he reached for the note, again without thinking about it. It was simple, one sentence, but it flowed into the mind of Ambrose Benedict-Matthews and rose there like the slow water behind a dam. He put the note down and turned to his newspaper. The news was already a week old, but he didn't mind. Ambrose turned to an article. The headline read, "Nurmi Sets Another World Record." He read it thoroughly, how the man had run ten miles in less than an hour, only a little bit more than fifty minutes to be exact. He was impressed by the man's fortitude but he was more impressed by the headline. "World Record," kept repeating itself, the water kept rising, the canyon was disappearing in blue water, "World Record," "I Can Give You What You Want," the water covered the ruins where ancient people used to live, the tall rock where young men used to watch for their enemies was disappearing in the cold blue water rising behind the dam, a Spaniard had written his passage on stone above pictures the Indios had drawn, all of it disappeared beneath the water, adobe turned to mud then silt then nothing but blue water, the canyon of Ambrose Benedict-Matthews' mind was fresh, blue, cold, and deeper than anyone expected.

"Is that what you want, a world record?"

Ambrose Benedict-Matthews heard the man before he saw him. The man had thin hair and his eyes were close together. He smiled and Ambrose was not alarmed.

"Excuse me?"

"That Paavo Nurmi, impressive isn't he?" The man was sitting across from Ambrose. He had not been asked to sit down, but Ambrose could not ask the man to leave. It would be rude, and besides the man was smiling. He seemed happy.

"My name is..." the man interrupted Ambrose.

"Ambrose Benedict-Matthews, born January 1873. That makes you fifty-five years old, fifty-six in two months or so, and you're still dreaming of world records, big block letters with your name running left to right. Now is that what you really want? I could give you that, but you're a bit past ripe, it would look odd, a man your age running to a world record."

"I need to go. It has been a long day."

"You relax Ambrose. Your fish will be here soon. They do a good job with the fish here."

"But—"

"I suppose world records aren't part of the plan, but all that money in your pocket, over fifty thousand. There is a thousand dollars for every year you've been alive. You figure your life is worth a thousand dollars a year. I think it's worth a lot more than that. I can give you what you want."

"I don't need anything. I'm perfectly happy and I would appreciate it if you would let me eat my dinner in peace. Thank you."

"So polite. I didn't know that about you. I figured you for less than polite, buying that piece of land from your son-in-law. You're a thief. That's the Ambrose I know. Giving him your daughter. That was a stroke of brilliance. If you were just a thief I wouldn't be here, but giving him your daughter and your last name. That's why I'm here."

"Please leave." Ambrose Benedict-Matthews was angry; the blood had risen in his neck and face.

"There he is. That's who I came to sit down with.

"I'll call the manager if you don't leave."

"The manager is on break. Woman on the third floor needed attending to while her husband was out. You and me Ambrose, I only need a minute. Your fish will be here soon. Don't much care for fish, but I hear they do a good job with it here. Once the fish arrives I'll leave you to your dinner. What say?"

"I have nothing to say to you."

"I'll do the talking Ambrose. You know that thousand acres you bought, real steal, giving up your daughter and all, I think that Ponce would have been happy with only the money, but you sealed that deal. Beautiful, your work." The man paused, his smile returned and he waited on what he was going to say, deliberate and patient, he waited there until he could see Ambrose asking him without really asking him.

"So about this time next year everything is going to go south. People will be jumping out of windows, and the wind, oh the wind will start and people will blow like tumbleweeds. Only a man with a deep stake in the earth gonna last through that wind. You and that thousand acres, you'll be fine, but how would you like to be extra fine? Things will be bad for going on ten years and then they'll get worse. People will think that things are all better, but there will be millions dead by the time the whole dance is through. I'm counting on somewhere near sixty million dead. Quite a haul, even for me. Right around when people start killing one another, that is when everyone will think that things are getting better, in the wallet, that is where they'll think things are better. They'll pretend to be sad about all the killing, and some of the good ones will be, but most of the people will start buying wool for socks, coats, blankets. They'll need a lot of wood for rifles, wood for crutches, wood to pack all those canned peaches and food, to build stretchers, put their flag on, and for coffins. They're gonna need a lot of wood to bury folks with. They'll need mountains too, where people can find gold and silver, pay for all that killing and buying. You can have all of it, the mountains with the gold and silver all the way down through the trees clear to them wooly maggots those people think so highly of. I don't like sheep, don't like fish, but look here comes the fish. You think about it Ambrose. You want to take me up on the offer all you gotta do is file the claim for that thousand acres, just list the seller and file the claim. You do that and I'll handle the rest. You do that and we'll talk terms later. Enjoy that fish. They say it's real fine."

One Particle of a Letter

Luke 16:17

Years from now a baby will be born. The child will not know Santa Rita, the road that still leads in, the iron gate and lock that blocks the road, protecting the homes of people who do not live there, the second homes of wealthy tourists built above the river and meadow. The child born years from now will be born in a room full of lights. There will be many witnesses at its birth, and the baby will carry a simple name from the Bible that no one will use. The child will call into a city with its cries of hunger, and that city will be called its home. There will be no record of how la communidad of Santa Rita is still carried in the child. We write this, the three of us through our father, and he brings it to this page, for the child born years from now, a marker like those set of stone on the llano's horizon, so that at dusk or in a storm, there is always a way home.

The people of Santa Rita did not like to be called Mexican. They had heard the stories of how this land was Spain. They had heard of Oñate who settled the terrenos of Nuevo Mexico in 1598. It will not matter to many that Oñate was a ruthless conquistador who punished the Acoma by chopping off their feet and cauterizing their wounds in boiling fat. It will not matter to them that Oñate was born in Zacatecas Mexico, not Spain. Here is the marker, the mojonera of stone that we leave for you. Oñate was married to the granddaughter of Moctezuma, the last of the Aztec kings. The conquistador came north with thousands of animals; his party stretched for miles through the desert. There were nearly two hundred families, some of them came north and settled Santa Rita. Of the families, most were already mestizos from over seventy years of intermarrying. There were over two hundred single men with Oñate and all of them were encouraged by the Franciscans among them to marry with the indigenous women they came across while traveling. Some of these newer families also came north and settled Santa Rita. In the party that Oñate led north to San Juan, there were indios that no one bothered to count. Of the uncounted, some made their way north. We pile these stones because the mothers are rarely counted. Their names are lost to those of the father and then to the husband's. We pile stones for the child that will be born years from now with a Spanish name. These dark stones on the horizon are left so that the child will know that Spain abandoned the people of Santa Rita. The volcanic stones will tell the child that Mexico abandoned the people of Santa Rita, and, later, so too did the United States. Here is a truth among the stones. The people of Santa Rita were unique in their abandonment. With very little, they survived the deep winters of the canyon. With only their communidad and sharing their gifts, their homes rose from the earth. Having only an old piece of paper and memory to mark their journey, they wove their own basket of words, intricate, unique, connected to the Spanish of their fathers and the many strands their mothers wove subtly into the basket that held their language.

Years from now a child will be born in a city, and the child will grow in that city and love money. The child will be taught, like a slow drip into the veins, that language is singular. The drug will enter the child's blood slowly, each drip of it, like words in a history book, will speak to the child. Each word will tell the child how there is only one way, but we leave these stones so that, later, you will know differently. The drip into the veins will make the child sleepy; the doctors will tell the child that there is something wrong and it must be cut away. The child will fall into sleep and wake later with a sharp pain, but the doctors will ease it. The child will walk away and, one day, find the scar left by what was cut away. There will be a smooth rise where the skin healed itself. There will be a thin pink gash of smooth raised skin, the only clue of what was. And how could the child have known? The doctors said it needed to be done; the doctors know how the body is supposed to work. How could the child have known what was being cut away? The child only knew what the doctors said, but here is another telling, piled into a ragged pyramid of stones, that centuries of storms have not tumbled. There are parts of Santa Rita that the child carries with it, parts the doctors could not find.

Santa Rita died, but there are pieces of her still with the people. We hold our old selves close to us at times, live in the memory of what youth was and only remember those times that were beautiful and those that were tragic. One by one, the in-between memories fade, and we are left with the parts of us that can save us. That is how Santa Rita is kept, in small pieces that can save us. Sometimes it is difficult to know where the past is carried, where there can be room for it in a world that fills everything in our lives. Where does Santa Rita survive among these things? The folds of the human heart do not hold it; they cannot carry what they have never loved. The child can't find it in a slant of November light because the child has never known the canyon light, only the open light of the open city. The part that can save us is written in us, a word that God has placed on our tongues. The word is invisible and hides among the perfectly pronounced words of English, the word lives on well water and a bit of bread it has carried with it, the word exists quietly, the word exists quietly like a piece of wood in a house where no fires are lit, the word makes its way out of us at times, it rises and flows, recedes and evaporates but always the word returns to us. The part of Santa Rita that people carry with them lives on the tongue, it is a particle of a letter, it is the tiniest of reeds in a great basket, the smallest of adobes in a great house. Years from now a baby will be born and given a name. For this child we pile stones that were scattered across the llano. The stones were dropped by our fathers. The stones were gathered by our mothers. The stones were piled here on the horizon so that the child will find its way at dusk or in the midst of a storm. Santa Rita exists on the tongue, a small particle of a letter that escapes and is heard and not recognized. The voice you hear belongs to your mother. It is also your father's voice. The particle of a letter that escapes is the adobe of Santa Rita. The sound you do not recognize is the river rising in spring. The awkwardness of the sound is rocks being piled. The child will be born and, one day, find a pink scar where something was cut away. The child will not know the origin of the missing part, but in time the word will rise on the child's tongue and the child will hear it clearly, a mother's voice, the part everyone forgot to count, will come through. The word survived on well water and a piece of bread it brought with it. The word is carried in your father's name and lives on

the tongue. The word is Spanish. The word is not Spanish.
The word is Tewa or Nahual. The word is Apache or Hopi.
The word was born in Spain. The word was born in Mexico.
The word was born in the Pueblos. The word is Santa Rita.
The word will start the child searching.

That Those Stepping In
May Behold the Light

Luke 8:16

Her body was autumn water, gold was reflected there, clear, smooth. The flat stone thrown from her hand trembled across the water and sank just short of the opposite shore. It had begun to snow, the season's first snow, a wet snow that clung to everything. Ramon placed another stone in her hand. The snow clung to their eyelids, melted there. It clung to their hands and foreheads and turned to water wherever it touched their skin. He wanted to hold her. Ramon touched her hand, took it in his and warmed it.

The bridge was old and made of timbers, and he took her beneath it, out of the snow. In the falling light her neck shone, wet beneath her long hair. Nonnatusia's hand came up to where her ivory necklace rested. She felt the smooth gift Ramon had carved for her and smiled toward him. They had spent their summer imagining this moment, the water at their feet, a V of geese moving south, the blackbirds on the riverbank singing in the season's first snow, aspen leaves lightly clicking against one another, the cottonwoods bent, twisted, reaching toward winter. Ramon took her in, held

Nonnatusia by the waist and kissed the water from her forehead. He reached for her hands, removed the warm flat stone she had been holding and skipped it the width of the river. He took both of her hands. Her palms were warm against his. He placed them on his chest and told her. Ramon leaned toward her. Nonnatusia closed her eyes and leaned into him. Her body was autumn light. Gold was reflected there.

> His vision from the constantly passing bars,
> has grown so weary that it cannot hold
> anything else. It seems to him there are
> a thousand bars; and behind the bars, no world
>
> As he paces in cramped circles, over and over,
> the movement of his powerful soft strides
> is like a ritual dance around a center
> in which a mighty will stands paralyzed.
>
> Only at times, the curtain of the pupils
> lifts, quietly—An image enters in,
> rushes down through the tensed, arrested muscles,
> plunges into the heart and is gone.

Ramon held Nonnatusia. Something opened inside of him; he kissed her again and felt his body open into a meadow. He was running. The grass was wet with dew and it licked at his legs as he ran. The image of Nonnatusia rushed into the heart of Ramon and was held there. The meadow was green with clover whose dark purple set itself against the lavender of the lirios. The image entered in and rushed through his tensed muscles, he placed her hands on his chest, something inside of him opened, and he was running. His vision was clear. There were no bars, only an open green of brome and clover. He kissed her again and the poem he had set to her, for a moment, was correct. There was no world. There was only Nonnatusia.

He was born in 1926, the year the poet had died of something in his blood. He was born in 1944, running, the meadow was green, the panther had broken its cage, there were no bars, his heart finally held the image, he ran, the dew wet grass was at his knees, the lirios scented the air, Nonnatusia leaned into him, her arms fell across his back and she held him, he was running, the center was broken, the dance was a straight line of flight, he had first loved her while listening to a poem about a caged panther, how many times his eyelids lifted to Nonnatusia and how many times her image had left him, like the panther, paralyzed, but he was running now, Nonnatusia's body was autumn water, soft and clear she flowed into and over Ramon, he loved her all along, there were bars, thousands of them transformed to dew wet brome and purple clover, the poem was right, his vision could hold nothing else, Nonnatusia, how many times had he said her name in the many seasons he had loved her, her name flowed like autumn water, her name ran in a straight fleeing dance, her name fled the bars of his many wishes and fell into his arms, he loved her, he loved her and leaned toward her ear where the snow had melted and he whispered it to her; kissing the sweet melted snow from her ear he felt the wetness on his lips, he kissed her again and tasted her on his lips.

Who of You If His Son or Bull
Fell Into a Well

Luke 14:5

In the spring of 1958, Samuel went into town and bought
a used blue truck. The truck was powder blue and ran
smoothly, though Samuel never took it over twenty-five
miles per hour. He had grown older. The five years since
Aresando had come home from the war were carried like
ten on Samuel's body. The five years had left him bent and
slow moving, his knuckles were knots of cartilage and bone,
his hair, which had always been white, was now thin. The
truck was quite a hit in Santa Rita. There were very few
people left, and the few who remained were mostly old like
Samuel. There was rumor that Dionicio was going to close
the cantina. The people said they had seen the lock Dionicio
had purchased, a padlock for the wooden door. Most of the
younger people had already moved to town and there was
no need for a school any longer. The one room schoolhouse
had been completely boarded up the year before. All the
children went to school with the nuns now; all of them had
English names and were learning about Columbus. Santa
Rita was dying slowly, and Samuel's new powder blue truck

breathed a bit of life back into the people. There were a few bets made as to whether Nomio could run faster than Samuel's truck, but mostly the people found life in the truck because it brought the news from town every evening.

In the early part of the day Elle would rise and pray for a bit and then go into the kitchen and share a cup of coffee with her husband. The two would discuss whatever Elle had prayed for and then make plans for the day. The plans were always quite simple. Their only concern was to determine where the two would park the truck that day. Usually they had to choose between the drug store and the old grocery store. The drug store was always a worthy spot because Samuel and Elle would find out who was sick by monitoring who entered, and if they got tired of sitting they could always go inside for ice cream. The only drawback to the drug store was that it was made of brick. Sometimes the two viejitos would choose one of the grocery stores, but their favorite was the old one at the center of town. There was plenty of action there, but the main attraction was that the store was made of adobe. The owner had used stucco and white paint on the outside, but the walls were still full of crickets. This windfall of gossip, together with the high traffic of the store, made this their favorite spot to park the powder blue Ford.

There were very few crickets in the town, but there were even fewer people in Santa Rita now, so the two viejitos had decided to follow the gossip as best they could. The store opened at seven a.m. and to account for driving time, the fifteen miles from Santa Rita, Samuel and Elle would usually leave their adobe home by five-thirty. This gave them plenty of time and assured them of the best spot to park, on the street, directly in front of the double doors to the store. It was in front of this store, shortly after Samuel had purchased the life-giving truck, that Elle noticed the ring of an averaged sized man who entered the store sometime before noon. It was the crickets who pointed out the man to her. The crickets mentioned that the man had come from Denver recently and that his wife was considerably younger. The crickets mentioned her by name and that is what caught Elle's attention, Malinche Santistevan-Matthews. She watched the man enter and paid close attention to him. She recognized his ring and knew immediately.

It was this knowledge that made the spot for that Sunday an easy choice. Elle ordered Samuel to park in front of the store. Here sole purpose was to point out Karl Varshant to her husband, whom she accused of being totally oblivious the last time the man with the ruby ring had entered the grocery store.

It wasn't that he was oblivious, though he felt that way more often now; his age was upon him now and he felt it fully. Samuel had been listening to a different set of crickets when Karl Varshant walked into the store. He was hoping to hear about Aresando, but the crickets were going on about a batch of tea that some woman was going to make for her husband. Samuel tried to tune the crickets out, but they seemed set on this one piece of news, apparently there was something in the mint. He had tried to get Elle's attention, but she told him to shut up because she was busy.

The man's name was Karl Varshant; Elle had gathered that much the day before. She also knew that the man was a war hero, a pilot who had shot down many planes during the second war. She could not put her finger on other parts of the story though. There was some disagreement among the crickets as to whether this was the same man that Apollonio had run off in 1944. That story was big news then, Elle remembered it. How there was no proof that Thomas

Barnes-Catlin had killed Ubaldo, but Apollonio had run him out of town anyway. The punishment had seemed harsh, since there was no proof, but so few people liked Catlin that no one protested. Catlin was old and heavy, with eyes that were too close together, but this new man was average and a little younger. Even the crickets could not clear up the mess, so Elle brought her aged husband to town that Sunday. Samuel had strict instructions to help clear up the confusion. She insisted that four ears were better than two, even if Samuel could barely hear anymore.

"When did Ubaldo die?"

"Que?"

"Ubaldo. When did he die?"

"Pues, a long time ago."

"I know that. When? What month?"

"It was before that Matthews ran off with all the lambs."

"Was there snow?"

"Are you going crazy?"

"I just want to know if there was news," she pointed toward the store, "when Ubaldo died."

"He died on the llano."

"And?"

"The llano. He died on the llano. Even you should know what that means."

"Take me home. I want to see if I can find someone that can answer a question without getting smart."

"The llano, there is no water on the llano, but his sheep were out there. Borregas have to have something to keep their mouths wet."

"Cabron, why didn't you just say that earlier?"

"I was strong back then. Remember? I even helped them carry Ubaldo up the mesa."

"Is that all you care about, how strong you used to be?

Haven't you been listening?"

"I was listening. You're the one who started asking about snow."

"This new one. He's Catlin."

"He is more than Catlin."

Karl Varshant was pleasant enough. No one spoke to him first, but when he addressed the people of the town, they smiled toward him and asked him about the car business. He never answered anyone. He just kept walking, his suits crisp and always well draped. Elle saw him in the mirror and hit Samuel in the ribs. The old man adjusted his mirror but could not see Varshant. Samuel reached for the rearview but Varshant had already passed them on the truck's passenger side. Elle hit Samuel again, but his eyes were already on the well-dressed man. Varshant wore a blue suit, a white handkerchief peaked out of the suit coat. His shoes were black and shiny, and he walked with the confidence of a rich man. He didn't bother going into the store. He walked past the blue truck and didn't look to either side. Varshant moved toward the corner. There was no traffic, but he stopped at the curb and was patient. He looked both directions and then took a second glance toward the lane he was entering. Samuel had thought it before he saw Varshant. That very morning over coffee, he had felt his heart fluttering like a bird that has flown into a window. He was a weak old man. Even his heart knew it, and that is when the thought first came to him. Samuel hated the way the man walked. Elle was searching in her purse for a rosary. The seat between the two was piled with Kleenex from her purse; Samuel saw that she wasn't paying attention. He reached down and turned the ignition. Elle, at first, did not look up, but when the vehicle lurched into gear and spun out from the curb she managed to let out a brief scream. It was too late. Samuel had the blue truck heading north in the southbound lane. Varshant tried to run, but it was as if he was too dignified to actually break his stride. The truck was in third gear and pushing 5000 r.p.m. when Samuel hit Varshant. To Samuel's surprise, the man in the blue suit did not try and jump out of the way. The grill of the truck hit Varshant with a heavy thud and the car salesman went down. Elle was screaming by now, but the truck kept rolling. Varshant's body sounded against the floorboards of the truck. There was a bump and the rear wheels of the powder blue truck were rolling smoothly again. Samuel looked in his rearview and saw Varshant lying in the street. The blue suit was torn at the chest and one of the arms was completely gone. Elle quit yelling long enough to realize what had just happened. She looked at Samuel and nodded. He had already put the truck in reverse, but his wife's nod was all he needed to ease the clutch out and hit the gas again. The truck lurched into the air as Varshant rolled beneath it for the second time. Samuel was sure that the man was dead, but he had put the truck in first gear for one more pass. Before he could take one last run at Varshant, two men came into the street and were looking over the limp blue suit.

Samuel lost his blue truck. The judge ordered that it be sold to pay for Varshant's medical bills, some broken ribs, a collapsed lung, a broken arm, and two broken legs. Had the man not covered his head with his broken arm, the judge assured Samuel that he would be on trial for murder, rather than attempted murder. There were many witnesses who testified that the old man had just gone nuts. Samuel knew better. It was the first good thing he had done in years. Varshant would be in a wheelchair for months, but the car salesman testified that Samuel was indeed the man who tried to kill him.

The blue truck brought life to Santa Rita for a while that summer. The news of Samuel's rampage was approaching legend. Apollonio visited his old friend and manager of the baseball team and assured Samuel that he had done the right thing. Apollonio promised to sing about Samuel for years to come, and this pleased the old man. Even the people in the town knew the words to Apollonio's corrido. Their favorite part of the song was when the judge asked Samuel if he had any comment or regrets and the driver of the powder blue Ford pick-up responded that he had two. His only regrets were not running Varshant over three times and not hitting Varshant with the wheels of the great powder blue truck.

Samuel never mentioned the nod that Elle had given him. He sat at his table and somehow looked younger and happier. The judge found him guilty and sentenced Samuel to seven years in prison. Samuel counted the years in his head. He could come home in seven years, 1965. Samuel shook his head and turned toward Elle and smiled knowingly. He did not last through autumn of the first year. He died in his sleep and Elle's prayer that she die first was not answered.

In the week before he died, Samuel had written Elle a letter. The letter was short and ended with Samuel telling Elle that he loved her. He told her that no matter what he was not like the worthless bull that watched as the coyotes circled the calf of the charlais.

By Endurance On Your Part

Luke 21:19

Aresando recognized the pain at the tips of his fingers, and in a few days they would be completely black. The October sun was weak as it rose. He had waited outside of town until Venus burned herself into the horizon of the San Juans. He had waited as the lights of town began to disappear into the day; he tried to count them as they expired. Aresando listened for the church bell to toll the morning mass and then rode into town.

Occasionally, like brief gusts of wind, he would think of his father. They had buried Samuel in the first days of August, and in the evening it rained in Santa Rita. His mother said that the rain was a good sign. It meant happiness. Aresando had not welcomed the rain, nor did he run from it like the others. He waited outside his parents' home and felt the rain. Instinctively he turned his palms toward the sky. Beneath his left eye he could feel the water running over his scar, the rain channeled into the deep groove of healed flesh and flowing toward his chin.

Elle called to him from the door, asked him to come inside, but she knew he would not enter. She turned away and walked into the empty kitchen. She glanced toward

Samuel's place at the table and saw where his elbows had worn away at the table's finish. Elle smiled briefly, the sound of rain on the tin roof was loud and meant happiness. She looked back toward the open door and into the small fenced yard. Aresando was gone, over the mesa she heard thunder like a door banging shut in a far off room, and then she heard Aresando's motorcycle, the loud drum of exhaust through its pipes. She waited there, looking through the open door, for the sound of the motorcycle to fade, for her only child to steer his motorcycle onto the muddy road and drive toward the cantina or toward town. Soon she would hear only the rain on the roof. She would listen to the sound of tin echoing through the house and remember when the three of them would sit at the table, trying to talk above the sound of rain against tin.

Two months had passed and Aresando thought of the August rain as he rode into town, how his mother only called to him once and did not persist. Apollonio's words were with him. "You weren't meant to stay right. You are something else now." Apollonio had told Aresando that when he first returned from the war, and the words had stayed with him, a snow that would not melt. He wanted to understand what the guitar player had told him.

He waited on the west side of the street to catch a little of the morning sun as it rose above the buildings of town. As the sun finally began to warm him, he thought of what he would tell Varshant. By now the car salesman had heard about the missing bricks. Aresando looked toward the Palace Hotel as Mr. De Leon unlocked the door. The old man did not wave or look up from his path. De Leon tried the same key twice and then groped through his ring of keys and tried another. Aresando recognized the man's movements, the way his hands shook, the way the keys seemed foreign in De Leon's hands. De Leon had been opening that same door for twenty years, but today he could not find the right key. Aresando watched him and knew that the lights on the highway had been De Leon's; the man was scared and that meant that Varshant was on his way.

Karl Varshant was still in a wheelchair and was being pushed down the street by one of Blaesilla's boys, the eldest. Aresando tried to make eye contact with the widow's son, but the boy's eyes were blank, a field of snow. The boy had lost weight and his cheeks had sunk toward his jaw. The boy looked tired, as though it was the wheelchair holding him up, rather than his legs. Varshant smiled and Aresando reached back and untied the saddlebags from the rear fender of his motorcycle. Aresando threw the bags over his shoulder and followed Varshant and the boy into the Palace Hotel. De Leon looked up from behind the desk and began to explain excitedly, but he stopped when he saw Aresando.

"Looks like our motorcycle riding friend here has something that's going to make you happy, De Leon."

De Leon smiled weakly and went into his office for another chair. The table was round and already had two chairs set. De Leon came in with the third and set it down for Aresando. Blaesilla's son helped Varshant from the wheelchair and onto his seat at the table. De Leon sat next to Varshant as the boy went and stood in the corner. Aresando sat across from Varshant, the saddlebags draped across the back of the chair.

"Your pops, one helluva driver. You come to try and finish the deal or do you have other deals in mind? Deals that have to do with my wife?"

"I found something on the road last night. I thought it might interest you."

"We are long past playing stupid, son. You know it's mine.

You just leave it there and walk out and we'll call it even."
Varshant pointed with his good arm toward the casts on his
legs and right arm then motioned toward the wheelchair
in the corner.

"I thought you said we were past playing stupid. You
know I'm not leaving."

"What do you want then, son? You want for me to just
hand her over?"

"I heard you liked to trade."

"Where did you hear that? What do you think De Leon,
am I a trader of goods and services?"

De Leon did not answer. He nodded toward Aresando
and then toward Varshant.

"Seems like you got Mr. De Leon all worked up, poor
fellow can't even talk. You should have heard him this
morning though, going on and on about how they wasn't
on the road. I thought my friend here was going to roll over
and die, you had him so scared."

"I'm not afraid. So why don't you quit with the stories
and deal."

"Why don't I just kill you right now? Take what I want?"

"Because you don't know how many packages I brought
with me. That's a big llano out there. Easy for two or three
of those taped packages to blend right in with the landscape
and never be found."

"I've always liked that about you people from Santa Rita,
all of you are hard nuts to crack. I've been working on it
for a long time now, but there is always someone that don't
bend the way I want them to."

"You got Malinche's dad to bend. That should have been
enough."

"Got the old man to bend too. I saw that Ambrose and
that Ponce come on my radar and I thought I had struck

gold. He really does think the king of Spain sent him here. He is so vain up there in his wood house that it was a nice pop fly for that greedy Ambrose. Just a real easy pop fly, get two of the seven out of the way. I thought the other five would be easy, but like I said, you folks are hard nuts to crack."

"We won't crack."

"It's written, son. You can't change what's written. Take a look at that kid in the corner. He can't get enough of the candy I'm selling. There's a whole bunch like him. And the men, well they just rolled up and forgot to work after Ambrose ran off. I was counting on you for anger and lust, but you're not normal; you're a bit too patient for my taste, but here you are."

"I'm done being angry and I'm here to trade because I love her, always have."

"Love. That's the thing with you people, always something perfect coming up and delaying my plans. I was counting on you for anger and lust, but your pops he took care of one of those. Two more, that's all I need Aresando. Maybe you envy what I've got and that leaves one."

"We take care of one another, share, feed one another, we took in the bueyeros, Nomio brings the dead home. You can't break us."

"It's written. Those two guitar players won't be around forever, and that old woman with the Holy Water, she's been protecting you too, but she'll pass someday. For some things I have more patience than you Aresando, but for my day to day business I sometimes run short."

"Let's get on with it then."

"You've got something that belongs to me. Four somethings I believe. Isn't that right Mr. De Leon?"

"Let Malinche go."

"Do you know that she has plans to kill me? Poison me like some cow. She doesn't know that poison is candy to me. Poison is my blood. You think I'll just let her go after she makes plans like that?"

"You're not letting her go. We're trading."

"That's right, a trade. All four and I'll let her make up her own mind. You think she'll choose you and that motorcycle over what I can give her. Yes, all four and we'll let her decide."

"Three."

"Three? You don't know your math."

"Three for Malinche and one for the widow's boy."

"They'll both pick me."

"Let Malinche choose and just let the boy go."

"I've got no use for the boy. These are just for show anyway, so the judge gets the right idea about how your pops hurt me with his blue truck. You can take the boy. His baby brother will take care of him. We'll let Malinche choose, but that will cost you four."

Aresando rose from the table and moved toward the door. As he walked he unbuckled the saddlebags and, one by one, placed all four packages on De Leon's counter. He motioned for the boy to follow and the widow's son walked from the dark corner of the hotel and followed Aresando into the October day. The boy looked at Aresando as both of them climbed on the motorcycle. The town had come to life while Aresando was inside. As his motorcycle rolled down the main street of town, some of the people from Santa Rita waved to him as they called out his name. He opened up the throttle on the Indian and the sound of it echoed off the buildings. He rode north, toward the edge of town and Blaesilla's house. She was in the yard hanging clothes when he pulled in. Patricio, her youngest, was at her side. The boy smiled at Aresando and then recognized his brother. Blaesilla ran toward her sunken son and Patricio followed her. The widow thanked Aresando and kissed him on the cheek. She was happy, the way Aresando remembered her in school. She was happy as when she and Malinche had raised the deer. Aresando said goodbye to them and turned the Indian toward the road. Patricio called out to him from behind and ran toward Aresando. Patricio ran alongside the motorcycle and handed a small box to Aresando. The boy did not wait for a reply; he turned in the dust of the yard and ran toward his mother and helped her take his brother into the house. The box had come from the nuns, the name of the elementary school, in silver letters, was written across the box. Aresando opened the box as he rode. Inside there was a small four-leaf clover pin. Aresando squinted at the pin and read it with his good eye. In gold letters the pin read 'Luck O' the Irish.' He placed the pin in his pocket and turned the bike onto the street and opened it up. He was beautiful, there in the autumn sun. He was made of wind as he rode toward Malinche's house.

About Seven Miles Distant

Luke 24:13

The palomina reached the deep snow of the first plateau
sometime after noon. Nomio rested her in an open field
of snow as he looked toward the ridge in the south. There
would be one final climb up to the ridge, and then he would
ride the seven miles to los brazos. On the ridge the trees
were wind-bent and short from too much snow. Nomio
knew he would make the ridge by nightfall, but he did not
want to spend the night where the wind came over the crest
of the mountain. He spoke to the palomina and she lunged
forward in the deep snow. The horse moved in short hops,
Nomio swaying on her back, in-sync with her movements.
Nomio was heading for the last high trees before the ridge.
It was a good campadero with an ojito that flowed from
beneath a huge rock. There would be a good windbreak
there. Nomio looked around for signs of the herd passing, but there was only snow. The palomina's breath came
quickly now as she worked through the drifts that broke at
her chest. The day was full of sun and there was no wind.
Nomio lowered his giant hat close to his eyes; he squinted
against the glare, and looked south through the steam that

rose from the palomina's body. With his eyes, through the vapor of the rising heat, he followed the stream to his right. In the deep snow the stream looked black and in the shadows where the snow met the water there was the dark blue where shadow and snow receded. The palomina's neck was foamed thick with sweat, and he pointed her toward the black mirror of water. The horse was tired, but Nomio did not let her drink too deeply. Once they had set up camp and her body had cooled he would lead her to the ojito and let her drink until she chose not to.

The snow beneath the spruce was not high and Nomio was able to clear a spot for a fire and his bed. He placed the saddle, upright, against the thickest of the trees, the horse blanket laid flat at the base of the saddle. From the tree he cut branches thick with sweet smelling needles and placed them where he would sleep. Nomio watched as the palomina made her way toward an open spot between the trees and began clearing snow with her hoof. The horse was patient, working until she found the short grass. As she ate, she continued to dig until she had cleared a spot that would hold her appetite. The palomina looked rested, her gold body sleek and muscular against the backdrop of evergreen, snow and shadow. Nomio walked up to her, ran his hand over the soft skin of her nose and mouth. The horse moved closer, smelling the grain from the saddlebags. The palomina's eyes were the color of the winter stream and Nomio saw himself reflected in them. He looked closely and saw where the black of her eye met the brown, where the brown formations of cataracts had begun to form across her pupils. She was his best horse, perhaps a little too old for what he was asking of her, but he could not imagine any other animal capable of carrying him.

Ramon had come to the high camps with Nomio fifteen

years earlier. They had stayed at this camp during the June of that year, before moving toward los brazos and then on to Blue Lake. There had been snow in the shadows of the trees and at the crest of the ridge. The two herders caught fish in the stream and buried them in the snow. There were seven herds from Santa Rita back then, and they had shared the fish with the other men. Nomio looked back toward the stream, almost invisible in the fading light. The palomina nudged him for more grain, but he held it back, promising her more in the morning. He looked again toward the crooked blackness that marked the water's course. He imagined the young Ramon lying at the edge of the stream, belly down, in the early summer grass. The dusk of the October evening was silent, but Nomio could hear Ramon's shouts from years before, how they carried through the open, the excited pitch of his young voice as he lifted that first, hand-caught, fish into the air.

Nomio broke dead branches from the trees and made a small fire. The night was cold and clear; the stars and planets shone in the sky. The people of Santa Rita would wonder about his camp that night. They would wonder if he had already found Ramon's body. The bueyeros had brought down their herds a few days earlier. Ramon's sheep were mixed in with one of the herds, and the man who watched over them had told him where he had last seen Ramon, walking toward the rounded summit of Brazos Peak. The herder who worked for the bueyeros told Nomio that Ramon had left a note, sealed in an empty coffee can, hanging from a stunted pino, near the campadero on the ridge.

In the light of the small fire, Nomio imagined what the note would say. Would it mention the third child? Would it talk about Nonnatusia leaving Santa Rita the week before the herds came down? Nomio was sure that the two loved each other. He had seen the way they smiled and believed that there was only truth in the way they looked at one another. Nonnatusia never removed the ivory necklace. Ramon, in his silence, after the loss of the third child, had never left her side. They had come up to the high camps together the summer afterward, to be alone and heal, Nomio was sure of that.

Everyone was surprised to see Nonnatusia during those last weeks of September. She had come down on foot, leading one of Ramon's horses, her belongings tied to the horse. She had come home in the evening, a Thursday, and went to the adobe she and Ramon shared without speaking to anyone. That night there had been smoke from the chimney, the moving light of a farol in the window. Nomio had come early the next morning, but the house was empty, the horse gone. At the grave between the two acequias there were cut lirios, fresh, placed in a clear jar that Nonnatusia had placed in the dirt. Nomio had thought to follow her, but that was not his place. The tracks led east. Instead, he rode to Ramon's camp and found his nephew silent and with the sheep. Ramon seemed happy. He told his uncle that Nonnatusia was tired of the lonely campaderos and had gone home early, that he would meet up with her when he brought his herd down. Nomio told him about the empty house and the tracks heading east toward the open llano and the paved road that led to the cities of the north and south. Ramon was silent at the news. Nomio offered to stay with the sheep while Ramon went down and looked for Nonnatusia. Ramon told his tio that it would be better if they left things the way they were. Ramon rose in the saddle, his back straight and to the sun. Down in the cañon they could hear the sound of the sheep as they moved toward water. Ramon thanked his uncle and rode down the hill to be with the herd.

Nomio covered himself with a wool blanket. He moved closer to the dying fire, waiting for it to become ashes. Later, he would bury the ashes and move his bed over the spot where the fire had been. He would wait for the fire to die down and then he would sleep. In the morning he would saddle his best horse and retrieve the body of his nephew, the herder Ramon Fernandez.

Why Did You Have To
Go Looking For Me

Luke 2:49

Dear Tio,

If there has been no wind you will have seen my tracks leading up the mountain. I am sure you saw them in the early part of the day before they had filled with light. My tracks leading away, at the hour you viewed them, must have looked dark and full of shadow. I assure you that they are not the dark footprints you have come to know.

We share the dreams and I will come to you in a dream when it is time to deliver me. I will enter the room of your dream softly and easily. I remember the dream of your abuelito coming to you, sitting on the edge of the bed and telling you, "no lo hagas mijo." That was a good dream, because you did not have to deliver him. Rather, he came to you from the other place, heaven I'm sure. In that dream he called you by your real name and asked you to forgive completely.

I never knew you when you were young, in the years after your father left. Apollonio says that you were an angry man, but I cannot imagine that of you. You are the best man I have ever known, and for that I thank you. You told me about your dream, how you blamed the bueyeros for your father leaving, how you were going to get even for his loss, for your mother's pain, for the loss of your baby sister. She died at a good time of day, there were birds singing, that is what you said. That must mean something, and that is why your abuelito came to you in the dream. "No lo hagas mijo." He was telling you to become the man you are now, to not carry the anger of loss. You listened to him and I am asking that you do the same for me. Do not follow me up the mountain. I will not be there. I will be three days distant by then, and even your great horse, or your shiny boots will not catch me. I'm not running. I am heading south to meet Nonnatusia. She will be waiting for me in the villages on the other side of the mountain. She will have a new wool blanket for me. She will bury the cold from my body and together we will be warm. I should tell you that Nonnatusia loves you too, so for her I am saying goodbye.

I can sometimes see myself in you, but mostly I am just an ordinary man who was always happy to be near you.

I am sorry that the sheep are mixed in with the bueyeros' herd. It will be an entire day sorting them out and for that I apologize. In the end maybe you can leave the herds together. The sheep will settle in together and become one herd. The sheep are not like us; they are happy where the herder leads them, and they remember the good places they have been. Some people say that they are dumb animals, that they share one mind and even that is not enough. You and I know better. People are more like the sheep than they care to admit. The only difference is that they are not happy with where the herder leads them. You are the greatest of the herders, but I am not the one who left the ninety-nine.

You do not need to go after me.

I fear that Santa Rita will be gone soon. There are so few people left, and those that remain are looking toward the lights of town. I had a dream about our home. It was like the dream of my tia, my bisabuelo, the horse, and my daughter. I'm remembering all those dreams now and I realize that I was the only one who was unhappy. In the dreams, especially the one where my daughter played the violin for me, those I dreamt of were always happy. That is how the dream of Santa Rita came to me. Things were out of season, but I'm looking back at the dreams now and realize that they were perfect. Santa Rita was covered in snow but the baseball team was playing. The snow was shades of green and blue in the tall trees, but the ditches were rising and the people were not afraid to get in the water. You were in the dream, your guitara de los dos cuernos, your shiny boots and enormous hat. There was snow drifted against the trees but everyone was dancing. Mana Virginia and Apollonio were dancing together, she was young and he was the way I remember him. She was made of earth and herbs and he was made of light. They danced together in the deep snow and everyone was happy. Aresando rode his motorcycle on the frozen road, he stood in the saddle as the light from Apollonio's body bounced from the snow and captured Aresando; he looked happy, beautiful, he was made of light the way stars are made of light. He was made of darkness too, but I could not see that. I could only see the stars. Tio, the people were dancing to your songs.

The palomina will be happy to turn toward home. I'm sure you will too. By evening you will reach the bridge where I first held Nonnatusia. Think of us there and in the other places our memory lives. I am not sure how to say goodbye. Men are not good at such things.

Nonnatusia asked me to give you a poem. The man who wrote it spoke German but he grew up in a place called Prague. I've read about this place in the books you brought me, but I cannot imagine it like I do Paris, the other place where he lived. He was a man with three homes and it seems that none of them fit him. I am from one home, one life. Therefore the poem that Nonnatusia and I leave you is perhaps, if only a bit, more hopeful than this idea of goodbye.

My dear Tio, I will see you again before I come to you in a dream. God Bless You.

> Let me, though, when again I have all around me
> the chaos of cities, the tangled
> skein of commotion, the blare of the traffic, alone,
> let me, above the most dense confusion,
> remember this sky and the darkening rim of the valley
> where the flock appeared, echoing, on its way home.
> Let my courage be like a rock,
> let the daily task of the shepherd seem possible to me,
> as he moves about and, throwing a stone to measure it,
> fixes the hem of his flock where it has grown ragged.
> His solemn unhurried steps, his contemplative body,
> his majesty when he stands: even today a god
> could secretly enter this form and not be diminished.

Look! Days Are Coming

Luke 23:29

We can see our mother and father. They are far off, like
small birds at the edge of a great meadow. They are not
alone, three walk with them, Santa Rita walks with them,
seven herders and two great horses walk with them, two
guitar players and a man who played piano walk with them,
an old woman who heals with her hands, her hands smell
of mint and she walks with them, a herd of memory that
emerges from the fog of the bosque walks with them, they
are moving south, my brother follows them and watches
over them, my brother is made of water, he is made of llano,
he is made of smoke, he is the one who shepherds them and
whistles back to us, his whistle carries like pollen in the
wind, it reaches my sister's ears and she dreams for them,
her dreams are like prayers, her dreams are light as a first
snow along an autumn river, her dreams float like music
from a small violin, her dreams drift like dreams into a
father's sleep, her dreams are as real as living, she kisses
her parents with her dreams, her eyes are dark and round,
her cheeks are enormous and her hair curls and curls and
falls across her back, she is the one who was dreamt, she

is made of dreams, her name means light and she walks with them, the light of her name, the light of her dream, she lets them imagine, and that is where I walk, slowly I walk with my parents, they sometimes think the same thing without speaking it and that is me, I am the voice that tells them they are together, I am made of Spain and oceans, I am made of Mexico and pyramids, I am made of mountains with cold blue lakes, I am made of adobe and memory, I am made of words that I leave for my father, the words are scattered stones, the words are smooth rocks born of rivers, the words are jagged and born of volcanoes, I leave the words on the open llano of my father's mind and he imagines them because my mother loves him, I leave the rocks and my mother blesses them with tears and prayers, she blesses them with love, she blesses them with the music of her voice and my father stacks them on the horizon, there are three of us that walk with them, there are horses and sheep that walk with them, the road is made of history, the meadows are made of memory, the mountains are made of hunger, the water is made of strength, the acequias and rivers are made of blood, the people that walk with them are made of bone and prayer, the people that walk with them are made of centuries, the people that walk with them are pieces of love, the sky is made of the same pieces, the rain is the pieces, the snow forms from the pieces of love, the snow falls onto the stones of the river, the snow and rain fall on the stones of the llano, my brother shepherds them toward the stones, my sister dreams them toward the stones, and three of us, two that were named and one that is known only to God end this story, we end this story the way a lamb being born in March ends its birth and begins its living.

Acknowledgments

Today, Santa Rita exists mostly in memory, the only road in blocked by an iron gate and a no trespassing sign. This book is for the people of Santa Rita. It is also for the people of every village and every town that knows the sensation of loss, but also of beauty and perseverance.

For her beauty and perseverance I am, forever, indebted to my beautiful and powerful wife, Michele. She is, and will always be, the personification of the powerful will that exists among our people.

To all of my family, especially my brothers and sisters, I offer heartfelt thanks.

I must also thank my parents, Alfonzo and Martha; together they have shown me how within every struggle there is the rarest and most precious thread of beauty.

A special thanks to the Trujillos, Michele's family, for their constant support and strong example of family and the many blessings that come with such a gift.

I would especially like to acknowledge Amos Abeyta and Edimundo Trujillo, two old friends who shared their stories with a young 'kid' who wanted nothing more than to listen. Their stories find their way into this telling, as does the spirit of both men. Thank you and may God Bless, always, the two of you.

To the many readers who helped me along the way, Koos Daley, Laura Pritchett, Mark Sanchez, Sister Rene Weeks, Herman Trujillo, Big Mike, my sister Anycia, my mother, and Michele who oversaw the creation of this book, thank you all for your generosity and help.

For their help with editing and research I would like to thank Koos Daley and Brittny McCarroll for their contributions and friendship.

Thank you to my wonderful friends, Carol & David, and Bill & Cynthia; Carol for your support and mentoring, David for the beautiful cover photography and constant support, Bill for his voice, his guidance and for believing in me and Cynthia for her generous comments on the fledgling pages of this manuscript.

Printed in the United States
98229LV00011B/17/A

9 780978 945688